"Ron Collins is one of our best hard science fiction writers—a novel from him is a major event. Enjoy!"

Robert J. Sawyer
Hugo Award-Winning Author of *Quantum Night*

WAKERS

By Ron Collins

SKYFOX
PUBLISHING
Science Fiction

Copyright

Wakers
© 2020 Ron Collins
All rights reserved

Cover Design by Ron Collins
© 2020 Ron Collins
All rights reserved
Cover Images: © Raggedstonedesign | Dreamstime.com

Skyfox Publishing

ISBN-10: 1-946176-21-4
ISBN-13: 978-1-946176-21-9

Other Work by Ron Collins

Stealing the Sun (6 Books)
Saga of the God-Touched Mage (8 Books)
The Knight Deception
The PEBA Diaries (2 books)

Collections

Tomorrow in All the Worlds
Picasso's Cat & Other Stories
Five Magics

Follow Ron at:
http://www.typosphere.com
Twitter: @roncollins13
Newsletter: http://typosphere.com/newsletter

For Lisa, as ultimately they all are

Learning Module 0.1: Pre-Wake Expectations

Welcome to Think Space, Mr. Montgomery.

Do not be afraid. You have not yet been given your full memory, so it is normal to feel anxiety or confusion. It's like this for all of you.

Waking happens in self-contained steps, most of which — for you — are now already complete. Your body has been rebuilt using stores of your DNA and is now in the final stages of confirmation. The connection and restart of your neural system is nearly complete.

We started with operations that control your involuntary functions: breathing, heartbeat, and others. You are operating fully in these categories. We then installed core elements of your personality from source files taken prior to your passing. When those were stable, we initiated activity of the finer tuned neural connections required for voluntary movement — the ability to control fingers and thumbs, for example.

When you are finally resuscitated, you will be able to raise your arms and lift glasses. Only minimal therapy will be required to ensure you have the nimbleness needed to feed yourself your own dinner.

Years of optimization philosophy and several cycles of trial and, unfortunately, error have brought us to this design — involuntary function, then personality and voluntary function prior to full memory — because experience with early cases proved that humans who were roused to immediate and full cognition had difficulty assimilating into our society.

Much has changed, after all.

Imagine how it would be for a businessman from the early 1800s to arrive fully formed in your own age.

This is among the reasons for our use of restraints.

Patient safety is always of the utmost concern, and without your full background installed, some Wakers exhibit violence spawning from their personality cores.

So do not fear. You are not alone.

This is also the reason for these Learning Modules, of which I am the first. We are here to help you thrive as we introduce you to this modern society.

So, relax. Enjoy your recovery.

It is only a matter of time before you will be back on your feet.

PROLOGUE

The thing Bexie Montgomery would remember most about the day he woke up was that the direct newsfeed was running a story about Kinji Hall, and her plan to put soup stands in every fashion shop in the world.

It was brilliant.

Women shop. Women get hungry, and when they are shopping for high fashion they want something sensible and chic, like soup.

Kinji Hall would make a mint.

She could charge two arms and a leg, and the women would still want more.

It was absolutely, honest-to-God brilliant.

The fact of this newsfeed became even more interesting later as Bexie discovered he couldn't remember anything else about coming awake.

No sensation of awareness.

No coming out of a gray fog or hearing a chorus of hallelujahs.

There was a heart monitor, he thought at one

point, though he didn't know if that was a false memory that came because waking made him think of a hospital room.

He couldn't remember the touch of a nurse or the feel of bedsheets on his naked body. Didn't even recall being concerned about the strangeness of having a voice in his head.

But he remembered the newsfeed distinctly.

Wondering who Kinji Hall was.

Asking himself how much it would cost to steal her away.

CHAPTER 1

"Come on, Maine, don't be weak."

He stood at the edge of the formation and stared down into the crystalline blue water below. Stone Canyon was beautiful here. The rock was warm from the midday sun. The sky above him was light blue, but just as deep as the water below. The breeze blew against his bare chest, making him shiver. His toes curled around sharp edges as he glanced at the gathering of kids in the clearing maybe fifteen meters below — at Beatrice in particular, who was dripping wet and made her one-piece look like something out of this world.

They'd gone out twice before, and already Maine knew he didn't want to lose her.

Lionel yelled up. "You gonna jump, man?"

He smiled. The weight of the riders' presence weighed in his mind.

He looked at the water.

He loved this moment, the anticipation, the feeling that came before the jump.

He loved the jump itself, too, as terrifying as it might be. He liked the sense of controlling his body as he plunged through space to fall hard into the water. Diving was a science as much as it was an art.

He liked the preparation.

He crushed on riding TS, too, of course. Beatrice's feed especially. It was fun to feel the endorphin rush sizzle as her body rose through the air, and that weightlessness moment at the top. But, while most people said they got the same buzz from a wire as when they did something themselves, Maine Parker had never been one to go along just to get along.

Maine preferred being the host rather than the rider.

He spotted the four columns of rock that lay below the surface to his right, and tracked the shallow sandbar further out in front of him.

The water was deep enough, but the leap had to be modulated just right. Hitting the sand would be disaster. Too close to the columns was tempting fate.

He bent his knees, and fear signatures from the riders amped.

They were going to like this.

Maine curled his toes, bent further, then launched.

Spread his arms.

Felt that moment of zero gravity, then tucked himself into a ball to rotate twice and twist as he came out of the tuck, looking for water, his hands in at first, then reaching.

The impact was sharp, a rush of white noise, then a muted silvery scrub of the cold water.

Gorgeous.

He glided to the bottom and pressed his feet against the silty floor, feeling the soft mud between his toes and the solid chill of deeper water. Opening his eyes, he was surprised to see the rocky column so close.

He kicked upward and broke the surface.

The gathering was hooting and hollering.

"That was sick!"

"Incredible!"

"I can't believe you did that!"

Lionel Burgess was literally lying on the sandy beach and writhing with put-on ecstasy.

Maine swam to the shoreline and stepped out of the water, feeling streams chill in the breeze over the warmth of the sun. He smiled, looking at Beatrice.

"I can do you better," she said.

"Oh, really?" Maine said.

Her smile flashed, and Maine knew she wasn't lying. "Link in, flyboy."

Then she was climbing the vine that lay over the rock, making her way barefoot over the sheer surface, climbing hand over hand like she'd been born to it, her legs driving her upward, her hair trailing in ringlets behind.

She came to the ridge, then stood, legs planted, arms dangling from lanky shoulders, the sun behind her framing her silhouette as she stood above them, flesh golden-brown against the endless blue of the cloudless sky.

Maine shaded his eyes.

What was she going to do?

Three flips? A twist?

He jumped into her wire to find her examining the rocks under the surface, felt the loose gravel of the cliff under her feet. She adjusted further right to align with the rocks. The movement made him clench his hands.

Beatrice was going to thread the columns, dive directly at the rocks, hoping to split the space between them.

"Come on, Beatrice," he said over the wire. *"Don't play with that."*

She laughed. *"If there's one thing you should know about me by now, baby, it's that I don't play."*

"You'll kill yourself."

"You don't trust me?"

She took a step back, then another.

Maine felt warm blips as others joined her TS.

They felt her plan just as he did.

"Stop it." Lionel ran toward the rock, his muscles glistening in the sun, sand still clinging to his back as he grabbed the vine to climb.

Maine watched him, knowing it was useless.

Beatrice took two steps and jumped.

He felt the fall, heard the cry of her voice with such clarity and such joy that for just one instant he forgot about the formations that lay below the surface.

He felt her entry, sensed the angle created by the speed of her run, the leg splayed off-kilter and out of control, the shin that crashed hard into rock, and the body, thin and arched as it sliced a path between two spires, then out into open water where friction finally slowed her pace.

Arms extended, legs together, chin tucked into his breastbone, he felt her rise, kicking upward.

As Beatrice broke the surface, Maine let out a breath.

As she approached the shoreline, he came out of the ride.

Lionel Burgess dropped from the cliff surface. "You scared me, girl! Don't you *ever* do that again."

"I thought you were dead," said Pammy Granier.

"What did you think?" she said to Maine.

Their eyes met. She smiled and shook water from her hair.

Everything about Beatrice Diaz was poetry.

She was a centimeter or two shorter than him, her eyes dark in the shade of the cliffs, her lips thin.

He held her by the shoulders.

"I think that was the most incredible thing I've ever seen."

Gently, he pulled her toward him.

She followed without resistance.

His face dropped toward hers, and she raised her lips to meet his.

Somewhere behind him his friends hooted and hollered. Lionel attempted to access his wire, but Maine shut it down. Some things were his, and his alone, and while he already knew Beatrice would never belong to anyone in particular, this moment, the heat of her body against his, the softness of her lips, the sense of electricity where her hand touched his shoulder — just like the moment where he saw Beatrice leaping, flying out in midair — was going to remain with him forever.

Learning Module 1.0: Think Space

More than a bit of controversy surrounds the origin of the term *Think Space* — or TS, as many cultures call it.

Some suggest it came from the original Brain Gang. Others point to Lin Wein, the cosmological philosopher who also drove the movement of social consciousness toward isolationism by presenting the arguments against space exploration that can be summed up in his famous quote: "We are spending thirty percent of our resources to go places where nothing exists."

Regardless, Think Space is a split world that occurs within the mind of each entity involved and is, in fact, a network of all individual networks where humans, machines, and artificial constructs each serve as unique nodes.

It is the fundamental center of human interaction.

As with most applications of communication theory, it works in three phases: identification, wherein one opens a conversation; contribution, wherein one contributes to that conversation in some meaningful fashion; and confirmation, wherein one receives the result of that input.

The physical manifestation of TS in human systems is the result of DNA channeling, an encoding process that begins before birth and embeds receivers into each person at the genetic level — creating sensitivity to fluctuations in quantum entanglements, the fractal nature of which allows a node to tune to any channel in free-space, or to develop their own channels over which they can then connect directly to any other node.

Sharing in this environment can be as complete, or as fragmented, as each participant desires.

CHAPTER 2

In darkness, with his heartbeat a dull thump that pounded between his ears, and feeling an edge of raw fear, Bexie Montgomery gasped for air and forced his eyes to open.

The room was bathed in soft light, tending toward blue. Lying in a still-paralyzed null space of lucid sleep, he deciphered rounded walls. Slits of windows placed high up. The floor, a light tile of some kind.

The smell was neutral.

He was warm.

Anxious people can hear their bodies working, a feminine voice said as the heartbeat faded.

Angela? Or had the voice been Pritzi?

Fuck it either way. He wasn't a goddamned pussy. He'd never been anxious a day in his life.

And who the hell were Angela or Pritzi, anyway?

"Seriously," he said with a thick tongue. "Someone tell me who the hell they think they are?"

A mechanical system the size of a mini fridge rolled to his bedside, the only sound the hum of its electronics. A ring of pale blue and green lights flashed from a control panel across its surface. Extending an arm, it disconnected cords from Bexie's bed.

Everything else was quiet.

Relaxing, he took in a large breath and blinked. Only then did he notice the sheets lying across his body, or in fact, the bed itself.

"Where am I?"

His voice was raw. His throat dry.

He needed to scratch his nose, but his arms wouldn't budge.

Glancing, he saw his hands were locked down, engulfed by bulbous cuffs of some composite material, white and made of a plasticky rubber, that were attached to rails that ran down each side of the bed.

They were warm, though, the cuffs, soft and fitted to his hands in ways that were anything but uncomfortable. He could sit here forever if he didn't have to scratch.

"How are you feeling, Mr. Montgomery?" the nurse said, stepping into view.

"Like a trillion bucks," Bexie replied without knowing why.

She was female. Young. Probably just out of school — thin, with short, dark hair swept off a smooth face. Her skin was dark, her features at least partially Asian. She wore a uniform that was white and pink, and seemed comfortable.

The nurse's lips curled upward in an expression Bexie thought was supposed to be a smile.

Yes, she was very young.

"Can I move my hands? I need to scratch my nose."

She used an edge of his sheet to do the deed for him.

A pair of sapphires were embedded into her earlobes — or maybe they were aquamarines. Bexie had never been good with gemology except to note the fact that jewelry made women happy for a while. But he noticed the stones as she leaned over to adjust his pillow because they flared with a series of flashes.

A line of the stones ran along the back of her skull to disappear under her hairline.

"Where am I?"

"You're in a resuscitation center in Geo-Span Medical Center, Mr. Montgomery. We're taking care to bring you up properly."

"Resuscitation center?" he replied. "Was I dead?"

Yes, he recalled. For some reason he was supposed to be dead.

She smiled again.

A holographic image appeared over the bed. Tables and charts.

The nurse waved a hand along a stream of color, then toggled a series of buttons.

"You're going to feel some movement in your arms and legs," she said. "It's a process of autonomous isometric exercises. Good for your new muscles. Keeps things optimal while you're processing. It means that once you're ready, you'll be able to stand up and move right away."

"Sounds great."

She pointed at several places in his chart.

A tension ran along his right arm, then his left, along his right leg, then the other. It didn't hurt. Just the opposite. It was like a rolling pin was being run up and down the long lengths of each extremity.

"Feels like a massage," he said.

Another smile came as she worked. Halfway, this time.

"What's your name?" Bexie asked.

"Julia Epsilon," she replied. "Of B-Ward."

"Well, Julia Epsilon of B-Ward, can I move my hands?"

"Your blood pressure is high, but you are doing well," she said. "I'll bring the doctor."

"I asked if I could use my hands."

"Soon," she said.

She glanced to the machine that had now moved to the foot of his bed. Bexie had been wrong before — rather than rolling, the thing was floating on a pad of air.

"Don't mind the tripid," she said. "They are going to test your nervous system and neural function."

As the nurse left, the machine ran two arms under the sheets.

He tried to pull away, but he found his legs, too, were locked in place by more of the cuffs.

A pair of instruments latched onto his feet, and he gasped as rivers of cold flowed up his legs.

"Jesus Christ," he said, bracing himself. "What the hell are you doing?"

The snakes stopped high up on his thighs, for which he was immensely relieved, then looped around his legs.

Another holo screen appeared, green lights

flashing.

The hair on his legs tingled in patterns across his thighs.

That's when the next chunk of memory dropped into place.

Past Wave Regrowth: The Contract

The room had reeked of leather and wood, with carpet that ate noise for breakfast. The air had been stale, the men aged.

He remembered contracts.

DNA. Simple swabs. A long day with his brain being scanned.

The smell of salt.

Goodbyes with work teams during his last day at the office. Email and video notes. Renee's very vigorous going-away present later that evening.

And finally, he remembered his bank accounts — yes.

He remembered them.

He was thirty-nine when the diagnosis came.

He remembered not believing it.

Bexie Montgomery was not a man who came down with a terminal disease. The all-powerful curator of Creutzfeldt-Jakob — an ugly, degenerative brain infection — hadn't gotten the message, though.

Blurred vision. Headaches. An inability to sleep.

"You're not going to beat this, Bexie," the doctor said. "Weeks, maybe months. Not years."

He was not a man without contacts, however.

He remembered Dr. Michela Angelic, who had perfected a stripping process that could save a person's brain patterns — personality, cognitive paths, and lived memories — but who had not yet published because she still needed to work out the back end of the technology.

Bexie understood her goal, though.

Clone and upload. Grow your own body, load your own mind.

He remembered discussions of risk.

That was his thing, after all — what separated him from the rest.

He enjoyed looking at a map of the moment and seeing probabilities. He prided himself in being able to parse reckless steps from those that were simply high-return events. Bexie Montgomery was a man who understood the value proposition of risk and benefit, a man who made a living seeing opportunities where others missed them.

He enjoyed making the right bets.

Bexie blinked with the impact of the memory.

He licked his lips and felt the stubble of growth along his upper lip.

He took several deep breaths.

With the nurse gone, he was alone, feeling the autonomous exercisers work through his legs and then up to his arms again.

At his feet, the tripid retracted probes.

"What year is it?" he asked the machine, as if it would respond.

"2372," it replied.

He gave an involuntary chuff of laughter.

"Holy shit," he said.

More than three hundred years.

He crunched numbers.

Assuming his pile could double every decade, Bexie was a gazillionaire many times over.

His laughter then was real.

Holy Mother of All that Was or Was Not Holy…

He had won.

He clenched his fists. Pressed his feet hard into the foot of the bed.

"Holy shit," he said again. "It goddamned worked!"

Or had he?

Was his money still there?

This is when the floating football entered the room.

It was white and spherical, with a row of lights flashing a rapid spectrum of colors. Sensors and short probes stuck out at all angles, but they were mostly rounded and bristly rather than angular and sharp, making the ball look like a puffer fish that floated in midair.

"Good morning, Mr. Montgomery," the thing said in a neutral voice that seemed to come from inside his mind like his heartbeat in the darkness had earlier. The phrase *Welcome to Think Space* came from somewhere. "I am your doctor. We are very happy to have you here."

Male, he thought. The voice was male. He strained to look left then right. He pulled on his restraints to no avail.

His heart pounded.

"What the hell?"

"I said we are very happy to have you here." The doctor hovered over his bed, blue lights pulsing slowly. "I see your blood pressure is up. How are you feeling overall?"

"I want out of here."

"You will be released when your recovery is complete."

"I've got things to do. I need to see my trustee."

"You will see a counselor from the Central Inspector's Office as we near your release."

"Central Inspector's Office? Am I a goddamned prisoner here? I want to see my trustee now."

"I admit I don't know what a trustee is, but the counselor will see you as you are ready to be released."

"This is bullshit. I can make things very unpleasant for you if I don't get my way."

"I don't understand."

Bexie shook his head. "Look at me, arguing with a goddamned robot."

He could believe a mechanical doctor wouldn't be programmed to understand banks and trustees, but he was talking about a goddamned boatload of money. He couldn't afford to take a cavalier attitude. And the fact was, his money was probably why he was in lockdown. Someone would want it. Someone with the wherewithal to lock him up.

"Can I at least get a real doctor here?" Bexie said.

"A human, you mean?" the doctor bot replied as it called up the same diagrams the nurse had.

"What the hell else would I mean?"

"Our nurses are made and deployed in such a way as to ensure our patients are comfortable in their presence, but we do not constrain our doctors to the physical limits of your human bodies. Perhaps we should consider doing that."

"Configured for our comfort?"

The doctor bot didn't respond, but Bexie's mind ran in several directions at once. *Clones?* he wondered. *Robots? Genetic engineering? AI interfaces?* She could be any of the above, he supposed. She looked human, but memories of progress along all these lines came flooding back to him. Even in his own time, robotics and cloning technologies had been combining to create entities that were so humanlike they could fool a person. All he could say right now was that Nurse Epsilon's touch was no different from anyone else's.

His gaze went to the doctor.

"I'm not joking. I want to talk to a real doctor."

"Your recovery is progressing well, Mr. Montgomery. I'll have a nurse explain the acclimation process shortly. Once we're certain of your body's ability to control itself, the restraints will be released. You need to rest, though. Give your body more time to settle in. In the meantime, I will prescribe the release of your next collection of learning modules."

"I don't want a goddamned learning module. I want my trustee."

The doctor left the room.

The nurse returned, and Bexie suddenly wondered what the doctor's comment had meant.

"We'll get you a conditioning nurse later today," Julia said aloud, her gaze flashing to the tripid and a pattern sequencing along her gem line. "But first let's get you a little more sleep."

The box rolled closer. An arm swabbed something over his leg.

He felt his consciousness begin to fade and remembered a name from before. "Hey, Julia Epsilon from Ward B," he said, sure he was slurring words. "Can you get Kinji Hall's cell phone for me?"

"Nothing named Kinji Hall works here," the nurse replied.

This confused him, but before he could decide why, the learning module's low rumbling voice filled his mind.

CHAPTER 3

The 400 was Maine Parker's race. He wanted to win.

Through the curve, he worked on his stride, focusing on his footsteps and his exhalations, ignoring the sounds from other runners behind him that echoed in the chasm of the facility, ignoring movements of other athletes training for other events, focusing only on a proper midfoot gait, on keeping his hands relaxed and down at waist level, his arms swinging, his body loping with what he hoped was fluid grace. The soles of his shoes sounded like sandpaper as they grazed the running surface. The weight of his body rocked back and forth as it transferred through his hips and up his thighs.

He checked the clock as he matched his breathing to that same gait, ignoring the burn of his muscles as he turned the corner and headed for the finish.

Behind him, Matt Reed and Lionel Burgess huffed harder as they stretched their own strides. They wouldn't catch him, though. They were basketball players moonlighting as runners, so they didn't understand what it took to win in a race, didn't understand that the opposition was really pain and fatigue, and that the challenge was really to bring discipline to bear against variance in your own stride that would cost you those fractions of a centimeter off each stride.

That's why the 400 was his race.

It was a race against yourself. A race where precision and practice and persistence met talent.

His monitor said he was within the parameters Coach Hedvitt had given him at their session before today's practice. His heart rate and oxygen exchange were good and getting stronger. A big kick would blow Coach H away.

He didn't have it, though. Not today.

He tripped the timer at 43.38, not bad for a kid with the Mercy North Academy. Good enough to win Zone, probably even good enough to make the Global Games. Still not good enough for himself, though.

Sub-43, he thought, hearing Coach H's voice inside his mind. *That's the target.*

"You, my friend," said Lionel as he grabbed his knees and sucked air after finishing, "are goddamned lightning in a pair of running shorts."

"That's da plan, right, Maine-man?" Matt added next, also grabbing for air.

"Yeah, that's da plan," Maine replied.

"My Maine-man is gonna just be cruising along and letting them all think they can win until the very end when he kicks in that last gear, and whoosh" —

Matt dropped into a caricature of a runner's squat — "he'll get all down there and be gone, gone, gone!"

Everyone laughed, including Maine.

Maine did his recovery and his stretches, then took his electrolytes and the protein builders that would repair microfractures in the cells of his muscles, then he went to the showers with the rest.

The steam was hot against his shoulders.

The water pressure at the school was better than at home. He liked the sharp feeling of water on his skin.

In the distance, the gang laughed at a joke.

Lionel, he thought. The guy was funny as hell.

He liked to be with the team. It kept his mind from wandering to "the problem." It was always there, though, hidden behind the moment. If he could have one wish — beyond being the fastest human being to ever run the 400 — it would be settling somewhere for good.

This time "the problem" was that the steward for Bay Pod 41, where the Parker family lived, was trying to get the community to agree to add a marine manufacturing site to their area, making it easier for people to receive boats they'd requested.

It didn't make a lot of sense to him — wait time for a boat was usually only a week or so anyway. Lots of people already put their boats in the bay. A factory here would just make it happen a little faster.

If the proposition succeeded, though, Bay Pod 41 would be rezoned, leaving the Parkers to find a new place.

Again.

Which would fucking suck.

His parents had worried about this for as long as he remembered, though *worried* was probably the wrong word there. The Parkers were about like everyone else, their record was solid, so it was never hard to find another zone.

But a move meant uncertainty while the request was processed. Although physically attending a high school wasn't much required anymore, swapping out his learning group meant he would have to suspend school while the move happened, which was both annoying and bothersome. The idea created anxiety.

He liked Mercy North as well as any, and the kids in his session seemed to like him. Coach Hedvitt was the best, too. If Maine had to, he would tram all the way across town to keep working with him. But now something bigger was at stake. Now, the first issue was Beatrice.

The idea of being separated was like a big piece of his chest had been ripped out.

"Maine?"

The coach's voice rose above everyone's laughter as he startled back to reality.

"Yes, Coach?"

"Come see me when you're done in there."

"All right."

"Mainey's in trouble." Lionel sang it as a tune. "Probably got caught looking over his shoulder on that last turn."

"Probably," Maine shot back. "But, I like seeing you, and lookin' behind me is the only way to take you in."

The team laughed.

Maine smiled, put his head under the stream of hot water to rinse one more time, then went to dry off.

He knew what the coach was going to say.

Because Coach H understood it wasn't really about winning for Maine Parker — or, at least, since it was a foregone conclusion that Maine was going to win every time he stepped onto the track, winning meant something more to him than crossing the finish line first.

Maine Parker was something special.

A world record was not out of the question.

The coach knew this.

So, what worried Maine as he dried off, stuffed his running clothes into the laundry, and put on his street clothes was that Coach H almost certainly knew he had coasted the last half of this practice sprint.

"Coach?" he said as he knocked on the door.

"Come on in, Maine." Coach Hedvitt motioned to a seat. "Shut the door."

Maine shut the door and took the seat.

Coach H was an old guy, probably forty. He had been a distance runner of some note when he was at school, but never good enough to progress far up the chain. He was still lean, though, still put in five kilometers a day.

Now he was sitting at his desk, looking at time sheets and metabolic charts on his data scan.

"Are you okay?" the coach said after Maine got settled.

"Sure, Coach."

"Really?" he said.

"I'm fine."

"Didn't look fine. Looked like you quit on me."

Maine stared straight ahead.

"You know how long it's been since a man set a world record in the 400?"

"Yes, sir."

"How long?"

"Fifty-three years, Coach."

"That's right. Shanghai, 2319. Lucifer Jones, running in the Global Games."

"42.82 seconds," Maine added. "With a headwind of 0.02 kilometers an hour. Bested Frenchie Tardiff's previous record by a full tenth."

"You ran 43.02 in the finals last year."

"I understand, Coach."

"No, Maine, I don't think you do."

Coach H's face got a set to it.

"That record lasted a hundred twenty years before Jones ran his time, right? Nobody without augmentation sets world records like that anymore. Nobody. Except maybe for you."

The coach let that sit for longer than Maine was comfortable with.

"You know when runners peak."

"Yeah, Coach, I know."

"Twenty-two," Coach H said anyway. "Maybe twenty-three. You drop a sub-forty-three before you're eighteen years old and every eye in the field will be on you, right?"

Maine wanted to say *I understand* one more time, but he knew how far that would go, knew the coach was on a roll and nothing would stop him now, so he sat quietly instead.

"You're a special runner, Maine. I know you know that. But you aren't breaking anything without putting in the work. So, here's the deal: You're not getting a shower ever again without giving me your best effort, you hear?"

"I ran a thirty-eight."

The coach put his hands together and rested on his elbows, waiting until Maine caught his eye before speaking again.

"I love you like a son, you know?"

"I know you do, Coach. I'm sorry. I'll do better tomorrow."

"You need help with anything, you know all you need to do is say the word and I'll be there. But when I see you on the track, I'm getting your best or you're not coming in."

"I'm sorry."

"So, let me ask again. Are you all right?"

"Yeah," he said. "I'm fine. Just got to get home."

"All right then. I'll see you tomorrow."

Maine stood up, shouldered his bag, and headed home.

CHAPTER 4

The next time he woke up, Bexie was in a different room — darkened, but clearly a small place, more hotel room than hospital bed, with a window view of the city at night.

New York?

Berlin?

He didn't recognize the skyline, but saw a huge metropolis out there, with lights extending across the horizon as far as he could see.

He wondered if he was even in the same building as he'd been in when he first woke — what kind of complex was this? Thoughts of his past life came back, memories of nights in penthouses and parties, days in boardrooms with champagne. The memories were intense enough to be real, but scant enough that he could feel holes in them.

He flashed on a college friend who punched a hole in drywall.

Music played in the background, piano and sax, a soft jazz beat that made him think of a night he'd spent in Louisiana signing a deal with ... someone. He couldn't remember who.

The air was warm, but fresh.

He moved his arm languidly, scratching the stubble that grew on his cheek.

With a burst of adrenaline, he came to a sudden full alert.

I'm free, he thought.

He sat upright to turn his palms up, then down.

He grasped the sheets pooled at his waist, then moved his legs.

They were free, too.

More snapped into place.

He was naked. The bed was a firm plank built off a rounded, concave wall on the left side of the bed. Body warmth radiated from the mattress. The room was comfortably small, maybe five meters long and four wide, kidney-shaped, and, yes, with a vibe that most definitely felt more like a hotel than a hospital.

Across the way the wall was lined with a mirror angled to reflect city lights on one side, and dim shadows from his upper torso on the other.

A door slid open, and a nurse entered.

The lights rose gently.

"You're awake," she said, coming to his side and calling up another set of holographic data forms.

"Julia?" He pulled the blanket up, intensely aware of his nakedness and surprised at the vulnerability he felt.

"Yes," she replied.

She looked the same. She wore the same pink and white uniform as before. He remembered the doctor bot saying nurses were "configured" to please humans. The idea of customized and configurable workforces came unbidden across his mind.

"You're the same nurse I spoke with when I first woke up?"

"Of course."

He hesitated, trying to piece together what had been going through his mind. "I thought maybe..."

Now that he was fully awake, he studied her features more closely.

What *had* he been thinking?

That the nursing staff was a collection of automatons? That they would all come in a standard model that looked like Julia?

"Are you a clone?" Bexie nearly said as Julia Epsilon inspected a readout glowing at the side of the bed.

Instead, though, he was sidetracked by the fact that now, in full light for the first time, he suddenly saw himself in the mirror.

"Jesus Christ!" he called out.

"Is something wrong?"

He ran his hand over his scalp. His dark hair was matted from the bed, but it was longish and supple, oddly shaped and shaggy enough he needed a haircut.

"No," he said. "Nothing's wrong."

He peered more closely. He was young. Really young.

"How old am I?"

"It is standard practice for Wakers to grow to their biological nineteenth year," Julia replied.

Nineteen. He laughed, then looked at the floor, wanting suddenly to stand up more than anything, but just as suddenly afraid of falling.

"Can I stand up?"

She offered her hand. "Let me help, but, yes, you should be capable of standing."

He took her hand, and with the other he gathered bedclothes to cover himself, then swung his legs over the edge.

The rug was soft under his feet. Julia's hand was warm and firm.

He planted his feet at shoulder width, then marveled at the simple joy of how it felt to lever himself upward. Her touch steadied him as he took a small step. Then another.

He straightened and stood taller — nearly a head above Julia, his shoulders back, and his lungs filling with a victorious breath.

"I'm letting go," he said.

A moment later he was standing on his own.

Then, Bexie Montgomery stared at the mirror.

He was thin and graceful.

There was barely any fat on his bones.

Soft light colored the high points of his muscles and left depressions in shadow. Even before his tone was fully established, those muscles were firmer than the Jell-O they'd been before. The dark skin of his face was unlined, and the flow of his body was perfect.

The ache that had been in his ancient knee was gone.

Prior to his disease, he had been aging as well as anyone could have asked — wrinkles at the corners of his eyes, and only a dash of silver barely showing at his temples— but now he was giddy, scanning left then right, marveling at the way his muscles flowed over his frame.

"Son of a bitch," he whispered. His disease. He glanced at Julia. "Am I cured?"

"Of your disease?"

"Yes, of course."

"You are healthy, Mr. Montgomery. Your resuscitation was completely successful."

A second nurse entered with a tray that held a bowl.

"Are you hungry?" Julia Epsilon asked as she entered information about his activity into a register she'd called up while he was gawking at himself.

"Yes," he replied as he sat back down into bed, suddenly more than hungry. *Son of a bitch*.

"We'll control your diet for the next few days, but then you can ask for what you want."

"What do I get now?" Before Julia responded, the second nurse drew nearer, and he smelled a universal aroma. "Chicken noodle?"

"Just like Grandma's, right?" Julia replied.

Bexie inhaled while the second nurse — who was young, like Julia, and who dressed similarly to Julia but also wore a pale blue sweater — placed the tray on a table next to the bed, then maneuvered it to his side.

"Smells outstanding," he said. He spooned some. "Not much here, though."

Julia replied as the second nurse left the room. "Your body has been sustained in a nutrient bath for many weeks now. We've found it best to introduce solid foods slowly."

"That makes a sad kind of sense, but I don't have

to like it."

"No." She chuckled. "You don't have to like it."

He ate a spoonful. It didn't quite carry the deep goodness of "real" chicken noodle soup, but it was tasty, warm, and just about the right level of salty. It made him feel better.

Bexie ate another spoonful.

"Be slow," Julia Epsilon said.

She pulled a new holo screen and jotted more information, he assumed about his dietary intake.

"Do you have any word on when I can see my trustee?" Bexie said.

"I don't have any news regarding that."

"What about the puffer fish?"

"Puffer fish?"

"The doctor," Bexie said. "They look like a puffer fish."

"Yes, I suppose they do," she said in a dry voice. "The doctor is a comprehensive, automated entity that operates fully in Think Space so it can provide health services on demand anywhere around the globe. It will load into any interface available for rapid response to a patient's needs. In our facility, the doctor fills one of many mobile nodes. They each have full access to the facility, though, so care is the same in all ways."

"Interesting," Bexie said.

He remembered a hundred meetings with a hundred inventors, having long debates about the best way to present automated services to paying customers.

"Are you finished with your soup?"

He held the bowl out for her.

"What can I do to get the doctor to authorize another bowl now?" he said with a grin.

"Excuse me?"

"I think I can make it worth your time if you can get the sawbones to authorize some more soup sooner than later."

"I don't understand," she said.

The nurse's expression made him think he'd broken protocol.

"Never mind," he said. "Just let the doctor know their work is going well, and that I'm still hungry."

"All right."

"Don't forget the part about their work going well. That's the magic phrase."

"I won't."

Julia took the tray to the doorway before turning back.

"You'll find clothes in the closet and dresser. Nothing stylish, I'm afraid, but they'll be warm enough."

"Thanks," he said.

Julia left.

Alone, Bexie ran his hand over his hair, feeling its silken smoothness, and the sensation of pressure on his skin. He stood again, then carefully padded to the window. The cityscape blazed with light, but there was a break in the distance, then more light. A river maybe? A park?

He would have to wait until sunrise to find out.

Tomorrow, he thought. First thing.

He was going to talk to his trustee or die trying.

He felt a warm sensation in the middle of his mind, almost a vibration, but not physical.

"You have received new learning modules." The voice inside his mind startled him. *"Would you like to absorb it now, or would you prefer to store it for later consumption?"*

"I'll take them now," he said, closing his eyes. "No time to waste."

An almost imperceptible silence passed before the module started.

Learning Module 2.0: Waker Tech

Welcome to 2372, Mr. Montgomery.

We are so happy to have you here. You are being hosted in the Geo-Span Medical Center in San Francisco, California. The world around you has dramatically changed.

The Waker process you are going through, for example, is the result of a happy combination of events that include the discoveries of several scientists and much hard work by Avalina Ricci, the simple librarian who made it her life's work to bring as many of you back to existence as possible.

Drs. Juanita Kong and Shidar Chippathi, for example, completed the mapping between the nervous system and each element of the brain. They had been working to allow better collaboration between work teams across great distances — work that, of course, is an underpinning to the expansion of Think Space.

You should also be aware of Maximo Huff and Lania Prevost, a pair of artificial intelligence algorithmists who led an entire generation of open system programmers known today as the Brain Gang. Their work served to develop our understanding of the complex workings of human thought processes that led into our current theory of multidimensional cognition.

Neither of them, of course, had Wakers in mind.

Huff's goal, which was widely celebrated in pop culture of the time, was to transcend the human experience by taking the "inner trip." Prevost's was more pragmatic, being simply to unleash a new wave of creativity that might raise the human existence to new heights.

In hindsight, Prevost — a transgender person of Lithuanian and Dutch heritage who had spent time in Mumbai and Ethiopia as a child — was the one whose vision was closest to the result, and it was her vision that led to the combination of their work with Kong and Chippathi's. She is the one who first understood how the new economics of product on demand could be affected by infinite supply.

Still, it's inappropriate to suggest that any of them saw their work as the root of Waker technology.

Our ability to resuscitate Wakers came primarily as a result of that simple librarian's visit to the digital museum at Seoul-dae, — or formally, Seoul National University — whose main repository is in Gwanak, a city often featured in media due to the architectural elegance of its hallways, and due to its extensive collection of ancient texts regarding the manipulation of genetic code that was so much in vogue during the chaotic years of the late 21st and 22nd centuries.

It was against this background that Ms. Ricci made her fateful research trip, booted up a machine that had been fallow for many years, and came upon several contracts such as yours.

This led her to repositories of DNA, as well as the locations of personality packages — those digital downloads that collect Wakers' minds, personalities, memories, and, some theologians still argue, their souls.

From that point forward, her efforts to have Wakers revived became a lifelong quest.

Without Avalina Ricci, you, Mr. Montgomery, would not be here.

As the module finished, Bexie heard a distant tone of music filtering into his consciousness. The aroma of soup made his stomach rumble.

When he opened his eyes he found he had moved to the bed and was wrapped in a blanket. A fresh bowl of soup sat on the table beside the bed.

I owe you one, Julia, he thought.

He glanced at the mirror again, confirming he was still young and letting his mind run over the ideas behind Think Space itself, about the acts that had to happen in order for him to be sitting here on this bed in San Francisco, with the calendar showing 2372.

Suddenly, he imagined Julia in ways he hadn't before.

She was young and attractive.

And, looking again to the mirror, he was too.

"The future is damned interesting," he said to himself as he reached for the bowl.

All he needed now was to figure out how to get to his money.

CHAPTER 5

Maine dropped his bag on the chair.

He pulled a plapple from the refrigerator unit and ate part of it. The fruit was a mix of apple and plum that Mom was particularly fond of these days. It was good, but not his favorite.

Not that he cared much.

Neither his mom, nor his dad, nor almost anyone else but Coach H could seem to understand that meals to him were simply something you ate in order to keep moving — though, admittedly, a good slab of brownie cake was an experience of epic proportion. Unfortunately, that kind of treat was not on the menu if he wanted to set records.

He walked through the house to find Mom linked-in on a musical.

The sound was off, but Maine stood at the doorway and touched the link so he could watch the dancers spin.

His angle made them look two-dimensional, but they would be real to Mom. She loved musicals, especially ones made back when she was a kid — the more flash, the better.

She sat in the middle chair today, an expression of content on her broad face, the muscles of her cheek twitching with a rhythm he couldn't hear.

Most days Mom and Dad spent their time on the same line, but today Dad was on one by himself, lying on his couch, as always. His set was latched onto a sea adventure that a lot of his friends were getting into—something that made Maine feel a tang of anger. *Find your own damned addiction*, he thought. He didn't like the idea of his dad wasting his time doing the same thing his friends were doing.

It just felt weird.

And it didn't bode well for tonight, either.

Probably meant dinner by himself and an awkward night studying.

Maine understood obsession, but his was more physical.

Through his TS, he flashed his favorite module of Lucifer Jones — the man's sprint to the world record — and admired the furious nature of his stride, the raw discipline of his form. Maine could watch that clip forever.

"Hey, kiddo," his dad said from his link. "How was your day?"

"Fine," Maine replied. "Did you hear anything from Zone Control?"

"Don't expect anything until tomorrow."

Maine grimaced, and opened the door to their second link-room.

At one time, his father had been trim, but he was

too big for much of anything now. Mom was better off — at least she could move on her own. But here was Dad, plugged into a program that had him crashing through waves and dealing with the rolling deck of an old wooden ship in his TS, his cheeks flushed, and a few beads of sweat rolling down his forehead, while in the physical he was amassing girth at an alarming rate.

"Did you at least make the pitch to the committee?"

The scenario froze in place, a wave stopping in midair as it crashed over the bow.

"I don't think it will help," his father said.

"You said you were going to do that, Dad."

"It's not going to matter, Maine. And we'll be fine either way."

"I like it here."

"You can find another school arrangement and another study session, or if you don't like the kids in the area we move to, you can stick with the ones you know. Just takes more tram time."

Maine sighed. To a degree his dad was right. Learning was self-driven, meaning the school wouldn't care about his transfer. Today he was attending Mercy North because his zone had aligned with that institution. All he'd need to do to transfer is advertise for another session in another place and start meeting with it. But there was more to it when you got to the details. A session was only as good as the people in it, and trading around was a lottery of its own type.

At least Dad wasn't sticking with the TS argument.

"It's not about the kids, Dad. You know that."

"There are track coaches everywhere, Maine."

"I like Coach H."

His dad pointed to him. "Look, son, you know most people don't think like you do with your running and your schooling. You're going to have to get that through your head if you want to be happy. You're just going to have to find a way to make it happen. I hope to hell that you get to that point soon."

"Yeah, I know."

Learning is fun, Dad, he thought. *Running is a blast.*

"Everyone needs a passion, but you're not going to be able to run all your life, and you've got to understand that life is about feeling good. The world doesn't care if you're the best runner in the world. It just wants you to be happy."

"Some people care," Maine said, already feeling the sameness of this argument.

"Fanatics." Dad waved a dismissive hand. "Or rebels, right? Off-gridders? Don't fall for the hype. Life in the old days was hard. Going to the Zone Control won't help us save the compartment, but we'll always have a place to live."

Maine stepped into the hallway and pressed the back of his head against the closed door as he chewed the last of the plapple with enough vigor he bit the inside of his cheek.

Dad was right.

Bay Pod 41 would get their boat plant, and his family would petition for a new compartment, and a week or two later something would either become available or be built and they would move on.

But Maine wasn't like that.

Why couldn't his dad see that?

Being competitive was hard when the entire world was designed to give people anything they wanted.

Sometimes kids even teased that if he didn't slow down with his talk about the world record, the Central Inspector's Office would be after him. No one plays a one-keyed piano, his mom had told him. And he saw that, too, though it wasn't consistent. Some passionate people struggled, others didn't. He saw it when Priss Arnett, who had always painted, started a collection of images that captured her teachers. She'd worked at a fever pitch until that point, then no more than three weeks later grew tired of it. From that point on, she talked about the latest news of this painter and that, but she never took up a brush again as far as he could tell.

It would never happen to him, though.

He promised.

Back in the kitchen, Maine dropped the fruit pit into the matter collector so the system would remanufacture its organic material into something else, then he went to his pod and lay on his bed, his feet propped on a big pillow with Mercy North's Panther icon stained into it.

His legs were tired in a good way.

He could still feel the burn of the track on the bottoms of his feet.

He wanted to finish the module on Shakespeare tonight because tomorrow was Wednesday, which meant the session was going to discuss it. He hadn't absorbed either *Macbeth* or *The Taming of the*

Shrew yet. If he didn't get those things done now, everyone would be ahead of him.

They would make good-natured fun of him, but he would know what they meant. Beatrice would care.

He smiled, thinking of her.

She had linked into his practice run and he had taken her on a ride that had her oohing and aahing in ways he would like to know a lot more about.

As far as he could tell, she experimented with about everything — always wanting to be on the edge, probably even more than Maine because, while he only pushed the boundaries when it came to running, Beatrice had no limits.

He'd wanted to be with her last month as she scaled the remanufacturing warehouse walls, but he didn't have the guts to do everything she did, nor would his coach appreciate the way she mixed the chemical, mental, and natural elements to go on her great runs of adventure.

Painting, quantum theory, social debate, free fall, and yes, even running — she was interested in it all.

And she could hang, too.

Beatrice, he thought, was gorgeous, smart, and full of interesting ways of putting things.

He lay back and toggled Think Space.

The Taming of the Shrew, he thought.

He wished it was *Romeo and Juliet*.

Past Wave Regrowth: Business Background

Bexie Montgomery came about his money the old-fashioned way, meaning he stole it from people who gave it to him willingly.

He was born in 2021 to lower-middle-class roots in New Jersey.

Went to school at Liberty Elementary, where the best that could be said was that, even then, it was obvious he had a talent for making things happen. In high school he joined every club on campus, which gave him reasons to avoid homework, but also made him popular enough that he always had someone to do it for him.

School was too goddamned boring for him, though.

Who really cared whether the Vietnam War started with the French, the Americans, or, for that matter, the freaking Mesopotamians?

It just didn't matter.

The Civil War was about a state's right to hold slaves. Done. World War I was triggered by the assassination of a prince gone wrong. Sure, it killed off a shit-ton of people. So what?

Why look backward when the world was moving ahead?

And English Lit.

Hell, if he needed to write a term paper, he could get Freddie Palanter to do it for a Snickers bar and an introduction to Gail Redfern. Not that Freddie could make it with Gail anyway, but who was Bexie to get in the way of a boy and his fantasies when profit was to be had?

Dreams, he came to understand, were the source of all desire.

So, no, school didn't teach him the things he wanted to learn.

Which were basically about profit and loss, return on investment, and a knack for knowing when it was time to cut and when it was time to run.

It didn't hurt that he was growing into the athletic frame he inherited from his father — a frame nearly two meters tall and properly proportioned at that — and that his eyes were deep puppy-dog brown, his skin was velvet smooth and colored the butternut tone other kids were beginning to stain on or bleach to. It didn't hurt, either, that his face was angular, and his cheekbones grew in as sharp as razors.

When his dad lost his construction job the family moved to Maryland, where Bexie tried a community college. But none of the kids helped him, and they weren't smart enough to get the grades he wanted anyway.

It was a bad situation all over, and he knew it even before he got caught in the office of Professor Stansi, uh, taking care of her business.

So, he started as a stock boy at Fesco and Sons — a small electronics warehouse with a walk-in front room. Seventy hours a week loading inventory, cleaning floors, and greeting customers.

This is where he learned to convince people they wanted the Excelsior A rather than the base model, because the company had added feature X-de-Y that let you track your dog, or your cat, or whatever animal the client happened to say they had. For pet haters, there was always the husband, wife, or significant other.

Instinctively, Bexie learned that if you made a man believe he was brilliant, he'd do about anything you wanted him to do.

And that women were the same, but more complex.

Women needed more convincing. More focus. They didn't start from a point of view that said their brilliance was a given, and every one of them was different.

Then there were the rest. Nonbinary, trans, layers of ethnic identities, class questions. The categories went on forever.

Ten seconds, though.

That was his goal.

He had ten seconds to figure out exactly what motivated any person who walked in the door.

Anything under ten seconds was a win, anything over was a loss.

Within a month he was playing .500 ball. A year later that figure was closer to .900.

Fesco promoted him to sales.

Two years later he swung a deal to lead the appliances department, and from there it took him only six months to take over an entire region — mostly because by that time he could, as the saying went, sell sand to a sheik in Saudi Arabia.

He "yes ma'amed" elderly ladies, and bullshitted kids.

He confided secrets to men, showing them things they knew were true until, finally, they would trust him with their car keys if he just asked.

He could smell a cheapskate coming from all the way across town, and would whisper conspiratorial comments to them. *Paying a little more isn't always best*, he'd agree. *To hell with the service contract — you know that these fucking engineers are just designing things to last exactly one day past the warranty anyway.* He'd lean into the conspiracy theorists. *You're dumb as dirt if you buy anything more than a barebones system.* He'd agree with the garden-variety skinflint. *And, yeah, just give me a call when this one wears out and we'll hook you up with another that will probably be even cheaper in a year.*

And women.

Ah, women.

Watching him in a bar in the early days was like watching a magician. You knew he was hiding something, but you could never see it. A grin here or a touch there. A joke. A confession. A comment about her friend. Whatever it seemed to call for, Bexie Montgomery had the knack.

The money he threw around in the early days wasn't as extravagant as he would eventually become known for, but it wasn't shoe change, either.

At twenty-nine he was a regional director.

At thirty-one an executive vice president.

Two years later he closed the deal that merged Fesco with a Chinese manufacturing facility and a Syrian distribution giant, creating Montgomery Industrial Corp, and expanding outside electronics to become the eighth largest distributor of product in the world.

He did engagements at top business conferences, and the paparazzi, of course, followed him like he was a Corporate Rock Star. Magazine reporters lined up for months in advance hoping for exclusives, which he would grant as long as he could control their message and imagery, focusing, for example, on photos like ones that had him escorting Trina Hallwedge to the Academy Awards.

She had lost, but the consolation sex had gone well past unforgettable.

A year later Montgomery Industrial was the number 4 distributor across the globe.

Six months later they bought number 1.

Not that life was perfect.

His dad passed that year, and he had to put his mom in a care facility the year after. He fought a stomach disease a while before agreeing to a stem cell procedure to replace his stomach lining, and then there was the dual paternity case brought on by the N'Taito twins.

On the one hand, the case was embarrassing, on the other, it said he had it in him.

He milked it for everything it was worth while he was dealing with Prince Ricard of Monaco. The kid basically challenged Bexie to a chick-fest, a two-week spree that left the female population of the French Riviera in ruins and saw the principality agree to a twenty-seven-trillion-dollar deal with Montgomery Industrial, after which Prince Ricard declared the challenge a standoff.

"We'll have to have a rematch when the contract runs out," the prince was quoted as saying.

Privately, Bexie, closer to forty than thirty, didn't

know if he could handle another bout with the twenty-five-year-old, but he said he was willing to die trying.

The press sopped it up, and so did the prince.

CHAPTER 6

"...Human-run companies could not compete, and soon came what is now known as the Great Collapse.

Unlike business models that created goods for consumption, this product automated workforces that could operate forever, that came with a single expenditure, and that did not consume anything beyond energy.

When, finally, the fellowship of China and Russia..."

Bexie shut down the link and pushed the table hard to get it out of the way. It was made of some kind of black composite as heavy as stone. The table juddered with a loud screech.

"This is bullshit!"

He was in a learning chamber — an oblong room of moderate size with curved walls that were barren and painted white so that the room had space to convey immersive, panoramic images and the situations around various elements of history. The flooring was a beige carpet of some type, the ceiling rounded and lined with acoustic tiles. Now the space around him was so quiet the room seemed to suddenly close in on him. Sweat pooled at his armpits, and the air tasted stale.

Winnie, his guide, stood a short distance away, serene as always, in a dress with a purple top that deepened to indigo at the long skirt. The waist was cinched with a simple belt. Her dark hair fell in a wave over her face, growing so naturally from the organic material of her scalp, but designed that way, perfect, he thought. Too perfect.

He had come to understand what Winnie was, a bio-int, a biological intelligence, a clone like Julia, but different from his nurse in that every cell in her body was infused with processing power — which helped her handle the massive holographic aspect of the chamber. As such, her movements were as smooth as a human's but sometimes — if processing power lagged during major projections — her sync was a perceptible moment offbeat.

Very far-future corporate, Bexie had thought at first introduction.

As Winnie came to stand beside Bexie's desk, her voice came through his direct feed.

"Why do you say this is bullshit, Mr. Montgomery?"

He pressed his hands hard against the tabletop.

The warmth to her smile felt condescending.

"Don't give me any of your 'that's so sweet,' crap," Bexie said. "You can't honestly expect me to believe things work like this."

"Several of our Wakers have required extra days

to absorb these examples of how your world has changed since you were last cogent."

"Robots?"

"If you want to call us that, though the term is considerably out of date."

"What would you call yourself?"

"It depends."

He clenched his teeth.

"As you've already determined, we are a collection of mechanical, virtual, and biological devices that perform all the work that goes into supplying nearly any fundamental demand a human being might have. Our experiences span a wide range from true mechanicals to integrated clone and artificial intelligences. Which of us do you want to talk about?"

"And you're telling me there is no money?"

"*Robots* require no payment, sir."

"No credit? No loans?"

"When a human wants something — or a human clone, for that matter." Winnie paused for effect. "They merely request it and the proper manufacturing entity will deliver it."

"Bullshit."

Winnie said nothing.

"The Middle East alone would fight to the death before giving each other the time of day, better yet join a centralized economy."

"The people of the land you knew as the Middle East now exist in shared spaces designed to layer over one another."

"So, they each live on their own holy ground?"

"Yes. There are still skirmishes, but they live in

separate layers in Think Space at least, and the CIO has removed certain weapon systems from existence, so the intensity of conflict has been reduced."

Bexie stood up and paced to get rid of pent-up energy. After a moment he stopped and pressed his hands against the projection room's hard walls, feeling it for the prison it still was.

"What if everyone in the world wanted a fifty-carat diamond?"

"It is unlikely that everyone will want a fifty-carat diamond at the same time."

"Humor me, Winnie. Let's say they did."

"Then they would be made."

"How?"

"Either matter generators or pure harvesting of existing resources. A large quantity of diamonds still exists in the natural environment, after all."

"Yes, yes. But you're saying that if resources were depleted, the system would just make more."

"Yes."

"Atoms in, anything out."

"Exactly. Of course, once people have access to everything, they often find they need very little."

Bexie shrugged. "Sure. Oversupply chokes demand. But not everything that can be desired is something that can be built."

"You mean something like land?"

"Exactly."

"Human land consumption is managed by zones and its use is voted on by all affected members."

"That's socialism."

"If you say so, sir."

"So, who gets to be Stalin?"

"It's very democratic, Mr. Montgomery. Everyone gets a vote, and every vote counts the same."

"Jesus."

Bexie leaned into the wall, feeling its smooth projection contours rounding against his muscles.

This *was* a fucking nightmare.

It was a lie. It had to be. All of it.

He saw it in the way her eyes glimmered underneath that calm interior.

Someone was reviving the richest Wakers and bilking them of their cash.

Now it was his turn.

They were feeding him this tripe to get him off guard. The long con game, three-hundred-years-in-the-future style. Was it even 2372? Jesus, that would be sick.

He ran his hand over his forehead.

He had to get ahead of them. If he could get them off guard like they had him, maybe he could make some headway. When in doubt, take the simple answer, and the simplest way to do that was to follow the money.

"All right," he said, leaning back against the rounded wall and crossing his arms. "I give. But what about something like art?"

"Art exists everywhere."

"Let's talk about the Mona Lisa."

"All right."

"There's only one."

"That is correct, only one original. The Mona Lisa you are referring to is at the Wright Institute in the area known as Zimbabwe during your first lifetime.

Today we know it as the South African province of Katalla."

"Now we're getting somewhere. What if I want it? What would it cost to acquire it?"

"You would make a request, sir. And a manufacturing facility would make a duplicate within a few weeks."

"No. I want the original."

"The duplicate would be the same as the original in every way."

"Not in every way."

"Down to the atom."

"The duplicate would be different because it would not have been painted by Leonardo da Vinci."

"Since no entity in existence would be able to separate the two, that is not relevant."

Bexie tried not to laugh. "It is totally relevant if you're selling it to someone who cares about that."

Winnie remained silent for long enough to ensure he was done speaking.

"I think it is time we draw this session to a close, Mr. Montgomery. I'll have the nurses show you to your room. It would be good if you could exercise. We can start again tomorrow."

"What if I took it?" he said. "What if I go to Katalla and forcibly remove the Mona Lisa to keep it at my house?"

"That would be considered a conflict."

"And?"

"The Central Inspector would bring charges against you to a council of your peers for proper corrective action."

He sighed.

He wanted to argue further, but it wasn't going to be useful.

He needed to get some time alone.

He scanned the room and found nothing that could be used as a weapon.

He needed to think.

Someway, he had to get out.

"All right," Bexie said in a voice that was low enough to be a whisper, but strong enough to be a threat. "I'll see you tomorrow."

The door opened and four nurses entered the room. Only, they weren't nurses now, Bexie realized. They were muscle. Guards called in to corral the tempestuous child.

The only question that mattered was who the warden was.

Learning Module 12: Central Inspector

Good evening, Mr. Montgomery, I hope your day went well.

The following module has been moved up in the queue based on your request for information regarding the Central Inspector's Office, often abbreviated as CIO.

The CIO controls all requests and ensures they are routed to the optimal fabrication facility. It also monitors performance and ensures such facilities operate at full capacity. Since the middle of the twenty-third century, the entity has also managed certain elements of governance as needed to provide for safety and the overall well-being of the human public.

To understand the origin of this entity, it's helpful to see how three events intersected — specifically the development of Think Space, the development and use of universal fabricators, and the use of remote communications technology in the field of brain health.

The initial instances of the CIO came to be once humans were able to connect with each other, hence required stronger and more centralized elements to control privacy and personal security. At the same time, however, progress in the field of universal fabrication, of which the rudimentary 3-D printers of your time were the forerunners, resulted in the systems we see today — machines that strip hydrogen and water into their atomic components to use as raw materials to build anything from cars, airplanes, soup, apples, or any other substance that can be defined in a molecular fashion.

It was only natural to link fabricator technology through Think Space.

Once that was accomplished, a customer anywhere could request anything and it would be built to order and delivered based on optimal fabricator availability — a requirement that, again, required the expansion of the central controller's role. Your own company's work in the field of product distribution created the manual forerunners of these systems — methods to assess orders and provide resources to meet the request are critical for this service to work.

As fabricators became fully automated, the need for humans to manage any part of the process — take orders, create the product, and make any delivery — went away. These were mechanical processes, and the robots did them well.

They did, however, require an even stronger central coordinator.

The final stages in the evolution of central controllers into the CIO came as scientists studying communications and language acquisition, along with doctors dealing with brain chemistry issues, teamed with experts who were developing customized approaches to the utilization of genetic engineering.

Constance Ben, a twelve-year-old savant, discovered the method needed to use Think Space connections to splice elements of code into the temporal lobes, thereby — in her case — providing the patient the ability to speak any one of a couple dozen languages.

The ability to use Think Space to alter elements of the brain once again changed everything, and the powers of innovation are relentless.

Ideas built on ideas.

More remarkable science resulted from leveraging Think Space's new two-way interface. Doctors, for example, could change a person's brain chemistry to monitor issues like bipolar disorder and other forms of depression. Others used it as a delivery mechanism for brain-centric gene therapies.

As capabilities grew, so did pubic fears.

With costs either zero or minuscule, it was only a few years before governments around the world signed the famous Global Commonwealth Agreement, in which every nation in the world agreed to abide by common sets of priorities.

This was the origin of the Central Inspector's Office as we know it today.

CHAPTER 7

The next day Maine practiced in the morning.

He had been worried he would be too preoccupied with Beatrice to concentrate. She had let him into her TS, and now that he knew even more about how she thought, he admired even more about her, something that made him know she was someone special.

Beatrice Diaz was an enigma, a young woman with a seemingly infinite ability to focus on the moment, and complete lack of fear when it came to exploration.

Instead of being sidetracked, though, he found it easier to focus.

He wanted to be like her.

And to be like her was to stay in the moment.

Focus on getting his right jump out of the gate, on keeping form, on maintaining posture.

He ran a 43.12 on his second run, a number that was good, but when he and coach H walked through the 3-D stop-space replay together he realized he could have beaten. He'd been planting his foot maybe ten mils too far to the outside, causing his stride to have an almost unnoticeable torque that swung his right leg in a torsional loop across his core.

"That's probably two-tenths right there," the coach said.

Maine scratched his arm as he thought about that. "Two-tenths?"

"Maybe more."

Maine set his jaw. Even he could do that math.

Two-tenths, maybe more, was maybe a sub-43. More than sub-43, really. A lot more.

If he could remove that time, Maine would not only make the Global Games, but would clearly be a contender to win. And, of course, there was still the record.

He was young, and still developing, but finding those two-tenths in a mechanical loss — a technique issue — would mean the physical growth he expected would carry him to the very edges of that record.

He had a lot on his mind as he stepped off the tram and found his way back home.

The door opened for him.

His mom was standing at the kitchen sink, pulling a sandwich out of the dispenser. He understood the look on her face.

"When do we move?" he said as he put his athletic bag on the table.

"Two weeks, sweetie," his mom said.

He sighed and gave his head an imperceptible shake.

"Dad didn't argue, did he?"

She scoffed.

Maine scratched his forehead. Now that it was real, he felt the loss of Beatrice like a boot to the gut. He was seventeen, and Beatrice was a few weeks younger. He was eight months out from being able to ask for a place of his own without his parents being dead.

Locking his Think Space down, he laughed at himself for wondering whether Beatrice would move in with him if he killed both his parents right now.

Clearing his throat, he drew another breath.

"I'll be ready," he said as he passed his mom.

Then he went to watch Lucifer Jones on replay.

CHAPTER 8

Bexie Montgomery pressed his forehead against the window in his room.

This was getting nowhere.

He was working with a holographic entity that hovered over his bed like a futuristic Buddha but had been introduced to him as his guidance counselor.

Outside the window, the afternoon sun covered a San Francisco landscape that was comprised of architecture he was still getting familiar with — rounded buildings with parabolic profiles coated with what he now knew to be optimized solar surfaces. A series of bridges spanned water in the distance. He watched cars — or, as the learning modules said, chains of autopods — move along paths that built themselves as each pod progressed, then disassembled themselves to leave open park lands behind. Construction crews seemed to be working on at least three additions, and it looked like another skyscraper was bubbling up to the west.

And the people, Jesus. Below on the streets, people moved in waves that never seemed to stop.

He saw no way out the window, and even if he found one, a drop of twenty or so floors didn't seem like the optimum path to freedom.

He had a butter knife from this morning's breakfast stored away under his mattress and had been contemplating how he would use it on the counselor, but its appearance as a holo image blew that idea to shreds.

"Can you just humor me," Bexie said, trying to keep his voice light. "I want to see my trustee."

"As noted, the position known as trustee has become obsolete. Your financial accounts have been discontinued."

He fought the urge to pound his fist against the security glass.

"You can't take what's mine."

"Your accounts had no value."

"You're telling me I'm fucking broke?"

"You are as rich as everyone else." The Buddha's smile pissed him off enough he had to pause before he spoke again.

"How about I talk to the Central Inspector."

"I am your counselor."

"I don't want a goddamned counselor. I want to talk to the person who can release me."

"Your physical recovery is nearly complete," the counselor said. "I am fully authorized to recommend release as soon as you have absorbed the learning packets and are deemed able to successfully operate in our world."

"Bullshit."

Still standing at the window, he really did want to punch something.

A man materialized before him then, a boxer wearing red trunks with white stripes down the sides, and a pair of shoes laced up past the ankles. He danced before Bexie, ducking, bobbing, and motioning him to swing.

"Go ahead, fool. Take your best shot," the boxer said, his words muffled behind a mouth guard. "Float like a butterfly, sting like a bee!"

Bexie laughed. "What are you doing?" he said to the guide.

"I've done nothing."

The boxer hit him with a left hook to the ribs.

Bexie was curled into the fetal position before he hit the floor, gasping for breath, his vision melting in tears. He would have cursed, but air would not come into his body, and speech was impossible. He rolled onto his side, thinking he was going to puke up internal organs one at a time, starting with his liver, his pancreas, or whatever the hell was closest to his throat.

The boxer disappeared.

When, finally, a breath did get in, it was like inhaling a cheese grater. He was able to get to his hands and knees, though, eventually, and then take another merciful breath.

"Jesus, that hurt," he finally gasped.

"You'll need to learn how to control these things."

"Fuck you." Bexie managed to get to his feet. "Are you saying I punched myself?"

"That is a fair enough description."

"How the hell do you make a hologram that does

physical damage?"

"The technical details can be accessed through another learning module. But, yes, you can convey physical activity in such a way as the receiver's body creates sensation. I encourage you to discover it at your leisure, but the overview is that your visual system is tied to the rest of your nervous system. Optical input is processed, and the brain sends signals to each area of your body."

"That's goddamned crazy."

The counselor shrugged. "It's in the learning modules."

"Look," Bexie said, finally getting enough strength to think again. "I want to talk to a human being."

"That is inadvisable until you've completed your learning modules."

"Inadvisable by who?"

"The advisory levels are set by the Central Inspector's Office."

"Who is that?"

"It is not a who. It is the Central Inspector's Office."

The phrase *not a who* triggered a snippet of music inside Bexie's memory. The tune wasn't directly familiar to him but was clearly tied to the phrase *not a who*, which he found to be annoying because he couldn't determine why he remembered it or even where he remembered it from.

Still, the jingle clung to the inside of his mind and wouldn't go away.

"Are you well?" the holographic counselor said.

"Fucking ear worm," he said.

"Excuse me?"

"Nothing," Bexie said, laughing hard enough he felt his ribs ache. They were going to be bruised. "Who judges whether my completion of learning modules is 'successful'?"

"The Central Inspector's Office sets the standard of satisfaction. I am authorized to make release when those standards are met."

"Jesus," he said. "One minute you're a bunch of socialists, the next a bunch of fascists."

"Fascists?"

"Hitler. Nazis. World War II. I'm sure it's in your data banks somewhere."

"Fascism was broader than the Nazis," the counselor said. "If you intend to make such accusations, it would be best if you spend some time with those data banks yourself."

"I know what I'm talking about."

"If you did, you would not associate our process with such dictators."

"And what dictators would I be using instead?"

"This is not a joke, Mr. Montgomery. All needs for services to be provided by a government or corporation have been removed. People today can have whatever they want. You have no need to follow any orders from others and, likewise, no grounds to coerce others, either. How can the CIO be dictatorial when we automatons are the ones taking orders?"

"I order you to let me go."

"I cannot do that until you are prepared."

Bexie's grimace twisted into an out-of-control smile.

"You will be ready when you have completed the

program."

Bexie stared at the hologram, seeing through its translucence to the background of the room. The heat of midday sun spilled over the back of his neck, and the sensation of his ribs bruising radiated through his side.

His eyes narrowed, and he focused on Think Space.

Could this teacher hear his thoughts?

Maybe.

He still didn't believe a word of this, but there wasn't another game to play. Not unless he made his own, anyway, and the Central Inspector held all the cards right now. If Bexie Montgomery had learned anything in nearly forty years of prior life, it was that sometimes fighting the current just got you killed.

He had to learn how to use the equipment he was attached to.

Had to understand where the feeds came from and how to toggle them to his advantage. Had to learn enough to make it past the Central Inspector, whatever the hell that was, enough to get his ass out of this prison before it was too late.

"All right," Bexie said to the hologram. "Tell me what I need to do."

CHAPTER 9

The view outside the room just made Bexie mad anymore.

Same buildings. Same sky. Same people.

It was late afternoon now, and the sun cast sharp shadows eastward against the city's surface. What was going on out there? Bexie thought as he watched the city move. It felt like the city was an organism itself, its blood churning, always changing, impossible to understand.

Could he be wrong?

Was life out there truly as simple as the modules made it sound?

Ask and ye shall receive?

He watched machinery work.

The height of his room made the people too small to identify, but the learning modules said they were automated intelligences — robots, working in endless loops to make whatever world humans commanded. Same with transportation. Food services. Everything. Automated intelligence building things. Growing things. Delivering things.

Was centralization the answer?

He didn't believe it. Couldn't believe it. There were limits, he knew. Communications problems. Reliability issues. Hell, size constraints of atoms, for that matter. He remembered an engineer back when the calendar read 2060 telling him about molecular scanners and restrictions on information packaging that limited their fidelity to transfer data. Full automation was impossible.

Wasn't it?

Was it more likely the scientists of his time had gotten it all wrong, or that someone was Waking extravagantly rich people up to strip their accounts?

He still didn't know, but human nature said to bank on the latter.

Physically, mentally, and emotionally, though, he was tired of the energy it took to parse out all this information and keep his thoughts to himself at the same time. As best he could tell, Think Space seemed to be configurable, which meant he could make it harder on his keepers. As he progressed, he thought he was getting better at understanding how to shield himself.

It was bad form to broadcast everything you were thinking to everyone, anyway.

So, there was that. It was fair game to build shields.

Since he'd decided to swim with the tide, he'd progressed better over the past few days.

The Central Inspector had authorized a raw newsfeed to come into his Think Space, and he'd been working to get better at the interface all day.

He could receive easily now, though picking channels was tricky. Creating his own channel was harder, though, and he was still working at transmitting his own ideas.

He listened to a recording of a gathering in Argentina where people had come together for three days of singing and dancing. The story came as free-form experience with a 3-D sidecar for those who wanted to experience it without being there.

He did not want to experience that.

At all.

The door opened, and Julia came in carrying a glass of lemonade with — he was sure — a shot of gin. It was what he had been asking for each of the last three days, a drink he started many evenings with in his first life.

"Would you like a drink?" she said.

He checked the time: 5:45 PM. Same as always. Regimented.

"That would be great."

"You haven't ordered dinner, yet. Are you feeling well?"

"Yes, thanks," he said. "I'll do it in a minute."

Julia put his drink down and went back to the door, which slid open for her even though he knew it would not slide open for him.

Bexie picked up the glass and tilted it.

If this were an old-time thriller, maybe he would take a print off the glass and use it to trick a security reader. Then he could slip out through laser-beamed halls and crunch a few security guards. Then he would be free.

Unfortunately, this was not an old-time thriller.

He sipped his drink, then called up a channel, feeling the infinitesimally small bump in his mind that said he'd found what he was looking for, then pushed the thought of a tuna salad, tomato, and avocado dish.

A message came back as received.

He took a celebratory drink.

Simple. Reach out, make a connection.

Ask and ye shall receive. He shuddered.

A moment later Julia returned with his meal, cheerfully arranged on the plate. The smell of tuna and tomato combined to give him a fresh burst of energy.

"You were successful," she said.

"Slowly, but surely."

"Hey," he said as she turned to leave. He felt the presence of the open doorway but did his best to ignore it.

She stopped.

He came to stand close enough that she had to look up.

Close enough that he could smell the scent of her presence, almost feel the warmth of her body. He smiled.

Bexie Montgomery had always been good with people, but he generally preferred to be alone — or was, at least, happy to be so. He was a loner at heart — something other people might find hard to believe, but was true. In fact, this element of his personality may well be exactly *why* he was so good with people. He found he could step back from the moment better than most, and that stepping back let him dissociate from whatever was going on and therefore see more deeply into something he would call truth.

When someone said they wanted wine, for example, but then proceeded to sip the same glass all night as they slipped from conversation to conversation, Bexie saw them for the conniver they might or might not be, information he might be able to use to his advantage later. A person who needs a shield could be twisted, and he could never predict what would seep out of those people when certain pressures were applied.

But being alone and feeling lonely were two very different things.

Bexie had originally stopped Julia to see if she'd leave an exit path open.

But now, mostly, he just wanted her to stay.

"Would you like to join me?"

"Thank you, but I'm not supposed to."

"I won't tell."

She glanced to the door, and Bexie felt her uncertainty.

"It's okay," he said. "I don't want to get you in trouble. Would it be okay for you to show me around your quarters? Maybe just to let me stretch my legs a bit and give me a better idea of how things work here? All these learning modules have me really curious."

"We are not allowed to have patients join us," she replied.

"That makes sense, but I'm not really a patient anymore, right?"

Her indecision came as a frown that touched her eyebrows more than her lips.

"I'm not in any medical emergency, right? I'm just in this holding bin until I learn a bit more, and then they'll let me free."

"We are not allowed to take patients out without orders," she said.

He gave her his most genial expression, then reached up and, after she gave him a tentative smile, ran a finger over a coil of her hair.

"Don't you think we could find some way of working something out?"

Julia turned her eyes to his. Her lips parted, and she took a soft breath that made one corner of Bexie's lips curl.

She seemed to steel herself.

A natural heat stirred.

"Not without orders," she said.

Then she left quickly, and the door slid shut with a finality that left Bexie startled and suddenly not particularly hungry.

CHAPTER 10

Perhaps he was progressing.

His learning modules were changing, anyway, moving past day-to-day skills and into the history of progress since the time of his original upload. The Central Inspector's Office seemed to be focused on a few specific modules, as they kept coming up no matter what channels he acquired. Among them was a pod on the anti-space movement of the 2200s, specifically as regards to Lin Wein and his statement about spending so much to go somewhere nothing existed.

The message bothered him considerably.

"What do you think of the anti-space movement?" he asked Winnie.

"It was an important factor in how the world moved forward," the teacher replied.

"I absorbed a module on Lin Wein this morning."

"A hero of that movement, no doubt."

Bexie nodded, feeling his heart beat faster as he relived the 3-D experience of marches and protests the activist had sparked.

"I don't understand, though. His argument was flawed."

"Lin Wein's viewpoint is strongly accepted by society."

"Society was wrong, then."

The teacher waited.

"He said there was no economic value in pursuing space exploration, but even when I was alive, we were making good cash with space-based business. Zero G manufacturing, and some limited asteroid mining operations were both taking off. They took a lot of up-front capital, but the economics were pretty big once you overcame entry costs."

"Society felt that there were limitations on growth of space-based business given the extreme nature of distances involved."

"I see," Bexie said.

He felt deflection in the answer: a politician's answer to a businessman's question, which made sense, too.

There was more to this than someone wanted him to know.

He didn't think it was just him being paranoid, but it was all he could do to keep his attention on the next module Winnie pushed him into. It was a how-to flick that dealt with public transportation and personal energy use. But all the while, his mind kept playing with an idea, a thought, a question that bothered him throughout the day and was still bothering him as Julia escorted him back through the wide and well-lit corridors to his quarters.

Why, in this world of ultimate satisfaction of

every need, did someone feel the need to provide
such propaganda?

CHAPTER 11

Shoes off, socks on, Bexie stood next to the doorway, waiting.

He wanted to see more of the place, so he waited, checking his internal clock.

Julia would enter at 5:45 PM.

Exactly on time the doorway opened, and the nurse entered with his drink.

"Good afternoon, Mr. Montgomery," she said as she entered.

"Good evening," he said, trying to remain calm while excitement rose within him. The door slid shut as she came completely into the room. Yes, the delay was long enough, barely. "You can put that on the nightstand," he added.

Julia set his drink down and came back to the doorway.

"Will you be ordering dinner in Think Space again tonight?"

"But of course!"

"You're becoming quite adroit with it. We are

hoping you can be released in no time.”

“I appreciate that, though I wonder if that really means you’re just getting tired of me.”

Julia’s laugh had a softer edge to it these days.

“I enjoy taking care of you, Mr. Montgomery.”

“I appreciate it.”

“Can I get you anything else?”

“No, thank you.”

The door opened and she came forward.

He held his breath, blanking his mind such that he didn’t touch a channel. He understood security well enough to assume that if a channel went one way it often went the other just as well.

Julia passed him, and Bexie turned on one foot to step silently into the corridor behind her as the door closed. The motion was smooth, and apparently quiet.

Julia didn’t react. Just kept walking.

He let his breath out.

Had he pulled it off, or had Julia noticed his movement but chosen to remain implacable for some form of plausible deniability? In the end it didn’t matter. He didn’t have any intention of giving himself up. But standing there in the silence of the wide hallway, it would be nice to know if he had a cohort or not.

He followed Julia at a distance, stepping carefully.

As the other corridors were, this one was well lit, the floor a soft gray tile that was easy to walk on but made soft noise against his feet when he moved too fast. He’d expected an antiseptic odor to hang over the place, but instead there was nothing — a simple neutralness that made the whole place feel oddly boring despite a slowly changing mural along the left-side wall.

Bexie followed Julia at a distance, stepping carefully. The floor was cold against his stockinged feet. His muscles tensed, and after only a few seconds he realized he was already tiring out.

She traversed the corridor until it came to a double-wide opening that smelled of food.

The kitchen, he assumed.

He ducked into an alcove that housed another room as she took his tray into the area.

Focusing quickly down the hall, he saw what appeared to be a gate at the farthest end. Other rooms led off both sides of the passage, mostly closed. A nurse came from one, with a small tripid following along like a dog at her heel.

At least three openings suggested either nurse stations or generous crosswalks. Along the far wall of the closest was a section covered with lights, flat panels, and a holographic display.

Elevators, he thought.

He itched to check one out.

He heard footsteps coming from one of the openings and passing the kitchen. Without any other option, he opened the door to the room behind him, pleased to see that the lock on this door wasn't somehow keyed specifically to him.

The room beyond was dark.

As his eyes adjusted, he saw what had to be inactive doc bots laid out on shelves. The other half of the room was lined with storage cabinets. The doc bots worried him. Yes, they were inactive, but if he understood how they were assigned, the physician would be able to step into one at any moment.

He couldn't stay.

He could either make a play for the elevator or go back to his room.

The elevator was likely a fool's game, but Bexie wasn't going to be able to get back into his room without some luck, either. Getting caught in the hallway outside his room, though, felt like it wouldn't be as costly as being nabbed in the elevator.

He turned a few calculations and got the safe answer.

Without understanding more about the rest of the players, he'd take his small winnings and leave the table.

Swallowing hard, Bexie cracked the door open wide enough to see another nurse carrying something that looked like a small gun, but likely was just a hypodermic syringe filled with a dose of dark fluid.

He waited for the footsteps to die away.

When that happened, though, the sound of doors sliding open came from both directions at once.

His eyes, now adjusted to the dim lights, saw cords reaching from the wall to plug into the base of a series of different robotic equipment. Probably janitors or repair bots. Power lines, he figured. They were all connected to Think Space in some fashion, so the plug was probably not for communication, anyway.

What's one more thing that could go wrong?

Finally sensing a quiet moment, heart pounding, Bexie stepped into the corridor.

Then, without warning, the door across from him slid open and another nurse stepped through.

"Julia," he said, fighting an immediate need to run.

She stared at him. "What are you doing here, Mr. Montgomery?"

He gave a toothy smile.

"I followed you out here because I wanted to ask you a question, but then you were gone before I could chase you down, and I got lost so I decided to wait for you here."

"I see. Please do follow me back to your compartment."

"I will," Bexie said, pleased.

The nurse escorted him back to his room.

He watched her carefully as she progressed, but she gave no sign she didn't trust his story.

His door opened, and she let him enter.

"Thank you," Bexie said.

"You are welcome," Julia said.

She was quiet for a moment.

He went to the window and looked over the cityscape. The sun was setting, and the sky was vivid magenta. The city's lights just coming on below gave it an antiseptic appearance.

"Mr. Montgomery?"

"Yes, Julia?"

"You had a question to ask me?"

"What? Oh, yes. Uh, is there stock available if I order shrimp scampi?"

"I'm sure there is," she said.

"All right, then. That's what I'll order."

"Do you want me to process that, or do you still

want to use Think Space?"

"Think Space," he said. "If something goes wrong, I'll let you know."

Julia smiled. "Please do have an excellent evening, Mr. Montgomery."

The door slid shut behind her.

Learning Module 22: Laws of Control

The Three Laws of Robotics (often shortened to the Three Laws) were a set of rules devised in the twentieth century by science fiction author Isaac Asimov and later added to, expanded on, or adjusted by many others. These three rules formed the basis of all early work regarding the integration of human intelligence and automated intelligence.

The Three Laws are:

1. A robot may not injure a human being or, through inaction, allow a human being to come to harm.

2. A robot must obey the orders given to it by human beings, except where such orders would conflict with the first law.

3. A robot must protect its own existence as long as such protection does not conflict with the first or second laws.

To these, Asimov also added a fourth, or zeroth law, to precede the others:

0. A robot may not harm humanity, or, by inaction, allow humanity to come to harm.

The Central Inspector's Office has enacted this zeroth law in several situations, specifically in areas where risk is concerned. Risk is dangerous, after all. Risk is a behavioral pattern, and as such, can be managed.

The first case of note was the CIO's infamous decision to shut down all sources of nuclear power shortly after coming to full control. This decision caused considerable hardship in Russia, China, and Japan until the Central Inspector's Office replaced the lost power with the combination of solar and wind systems that supply most regions today.

Impacted humans complained that the action violated the covenant since it brought harm to human beings, but after considerable deliberation the CIO concluded that the code that controls the zeroth law allowed for and even required the decision as it was in the best interest of the whole, and so some sacrifices were to be expected from the individual as long as those sacrifices were not related to personal safety.

It was a nuanced argument, the first of many such nuanced arguments that led to the CIO's eventual practice of preemptive manipulation, the act of identifying people who showed reckless tendencies, then limiting their ability to follow thought streams that might lead them to high-risk activities, that served to protect individuals — and, by definition, humanity as a whole — from themselves.

The nuclear decision stood, and in this case, the power grid was operational within a few months.

Humanity applauded.

CHAPTER 12

The evening air was sharp and clear as Maine Parker strode toward the civic center where he would meet the group that comprised his current study session. A brief shower had cleared the air and, with the sun fading, phosphorescent lights cast a green tint to everything. There was never a lack of things to do in Los Angeles, and this early in the evening the sidewalk was filled with people heading to games, or plays, or dinner. Their voices carried in a din over the sounds of the city's inner workings, their strides created constant movement, their heads bobbing up and down in random waves.

Practice had ended an hour ago, and the muscles of his legs carried that pleasant deadness of recovery he liked so much. His shoulders were weary as he walked, feeling tender even under the light weight of the athletic bag he had thrown over his right side.

43:05 today.

He gave a heavy sigh, and the clean air of the city cut into him.

So close.

He kicked at a crack in the sidewalk, sending crumbling plasphalt skittering across the path. In some ways, five-hundredths off was worse than ten.

A pair of repair bots were working ahead of him, their hunched shapes lurching this way and that. Tram traffic flowed past in an endless stream, each shifting its course to avoid impact with the construction effort. The odor of the mix the bots were using to patch the walkway caught the back of his throat. By the time he returned, they'd have it repaired.

The session he worked with was a collection of twenty kids who got together every day to teach each other about things they had learned. Maine had been a part of six such groups over his past. They weren't hard to get into as long as it was obvious you wanted to learn something.

He liked this collective.

The idea that he would have to move away bothered him as he drew near.

The gang was active and smart. A fun group.

They all did their own projects, and today were going to gather to talk about Kaley Denning's work: the concept of drawing energy from quantum foam. She was comparing the possible energy scrape to the use of solar power today. It was probably why he noticed the pattern of heads bobbing up and down as he walked. Kaley had talked to him about it at the lake. Quantum foam, simplified, was particles of energy, appearing into the universe, then retreating away. For a minute, he pictured a sea of particles, bobbing up and down, into and out of the world. A quantum sea, he thought.

Silly.

Maine didn't think quantum foam would ever replace the sun as a true source of energy. It was too hard to mine, for one thing. And too dangerous for that matter. It would have to be done out in space, and the combination of the CIO and humanity had long ago concluded that space travel was a bad investment in human life.

But he enjoyed thinking about it.

Mostly, though, as he approached the center tonight, he hoped Beatrice would be there. On days when he trained, Maine usually attended the learning group through Think Space, but he didn't want to miss being with her.

He felt anxious, though.

Didn't know how to tell her he was moving.

He shook his free arm to relieve the stress, then gripped the shoulder harness of his bag with the other hand. His stride was long, and for just a moment he returned to Coach H's preaching from earlier in the day — picturing the swing of each leg and working to place his feet exactly where he wanted them to be. Precise. Perfect. The act cleared his mind and left him free to think about the words he would use.

He worried about how she might react.

What if she freaked out?

What if she didn't?

Which was worse, dealing with a distraught girlfriend, or facing the fact that she could write him off without a second thought?

"It's not fair."

But no one was listening to him.

He stepped through the center's glass panel doors and into the brightly lit hallway that led further in. The gang was there in the Haven room, as always, a place that was big enough for all of them and came equipped with a full suite of projectors and TS pools. He took a moment to activate his study log so Mercy North's monitors would register him in, then moved on.

The gathering noted his entrance.

"Hey," he said, scanning the room while he hefted the bag onto a tall table.

"She's not here yet, dude."

Calvin Jude, who the session knew as "Dr. Strangejude," was standing in a holographic representation of a strand of frog DNA, in which he had marked several elements for playback. Calvin had been interested in this for a couple months now, and the map had probably a hundred segments marked and listed. He appeared to be getting ready to splice in a new sequence somewhere, presumably to let a simulation run to see how his predefined mutation might change the creature's evolutionary path.

There was a reason for his nickname, after all.

"Who's not here?" Maine replied.

"Don't make me laugh. You know very well who isn't here. We all heard about you and Beatrice at Stone Canyon, man. News gets around."

Maine blushed.

He looked for Beatrice again, and he was still disappointed to not find her.

Maybe she wasn't even coming.

Or maybe she would just step in through Think Space — which would mean he'd wasted his time coming down here in person.

"You okay?" Calvin said as Maine took a seat. Kaley was at the center of the room, preparing.

"Yeah."

"You look down."

"Hmmm."

"Seriously, dude. You could block the sun. Wanna talk about it?"

"No, I don't want to talk about it."

"Don't want to talk about what, baby?" Beatrice's voice from behind him made Maine jump.

Crap.

Next, she would see that his palms were sweating.

He turned and immediately felt more anxiety at her closeness.

She was her same gorgeous self, wearing a loose-fitting blouse that fell off one shoulder to display an electric tattoo that snaked over her collarbone and up into the small of her neck. Her platform shoes accentuated her height. Her hair fell across the other shoulder. She smelled ... amazing.

Words fell out of his mouth like lumps of clay.

"I don't know how to say it, but I need to let you know that my parents lost their compartment. We're moving away."

"Oh, man." She paused, twisting her lips to one side as the information settled. "That sucks."

"I'm sorry."

She put her hand on his arm. "Are you all right?"

He shrugged. "I don't want to move."

"Why not?"

The offhand way she said it hurt him more than he thought it would.

Why not? he thought. *How about "because I don't want to have to travel into town every day to practice," or maybe try "I like this group really well," or maybe just "I love you and can't imagine not being with you?"*

He swallowed his anger and settled for: "Everything I'm interested in is here."

"What he means," Calvin said with a grin, "is that

it's going to be a lot harder getting into your pants if he doesn't live here."

Maine's cheeks grew warm. He held Beatrice's hand and walked a distance away so they could talk more directly.

"I'm sorry about him," he said. "That's *not* what I meant."

"So ... you don't want to get into my pants?"

"No ... I mean ... that's ..." Maine put his hand to his head. "I'm in trouble any way I answer that question, aren't I?"

Her shrug didn't seem like a definitive answer, but her expression was a mix of interest and amusement.

Maine's pulse rose into his throat.

"Look," he finally said. "You've got to think I'm the dumbest ass on the face of the planet. But all I can really say is that I want to be able to see you."

She reached up and kissed him on the cheek.

"It's okay." She gave him a close-lipped smile. "I don't think you're an ass at all. And we've got Think Space. My aunt and uncle have been living on different sides of the globe for three years. I'm sure we can find time."

"I was hoping for more than that."

"That's nice," she said.

"I mean it," he said, bringing his eyebrows together. "I want to be with you every day."

He had expected her to agree with him — at least to that point, anyway. He'd wanted her to say that the physical was better. Or maybe to push him away. Or get angry. Or ... well ... to do something. That was what he loved about her, after all. The fire that seemed to surround her, even when she was just sitting still. Her passion. The way she took every moment for exactly what it could be.

Instead Beatrice simply said, "We can make it work either way."

At least she looked glum.

"Maybe you'll find another pod close by," she added. "Or at least maybe we can move our sessions closer? And either way we can still meet here at the club sometimes."

He took a big breath to help release tension.

"Between you and Coach H, I'd be on a tram for half of my life."

He considered his next comments carefully.

Looking into her eyes then felt just as if he were standing at the edge of the cliff at the lake, looking into a bottom of nothing but rocky spikes. He most definitely didn't want to tram both ways, but the words he'd been practicing ever since practice had ended seemed to stick in his mouth.

"I've been thinking about starting out on my own."

"Leave your parents?"

"Yeah."

He hoped the tone of his voice would come off as the kind of independent toughness that would draw a rise from her. She was a daredevil, after all. The idea of having a brash side was something he wanted to cultivate.

"I was wondering if maybe you might want to come with me?"

Beatrice made her lips into a thin line.

"We could make it, you know. On our own."

"I don't know if that's very smart."

He frowned again. "What do you mean?"

"Living on scraps?"

"We can figure something out."

"Seriously, Maine. Kids on their own ... I mean, you can't order what you want until you're eighteen. So really you just wind up sleeping in the communal centers."

He didn't say anything for several moments.

She was right, but he hadn't seen it as a problem. Finding space in a community shelter wouldn't be hard — though he understood some would find it less than appealing. He wasn't, however, turning eighteen for eight months, and she was still a few weeks behind. The units were their only real choice. But of all the things Beatrice could have said to the idea of running away together, practical advice on living conditions was not what he would ever have predicted.

"Didn't you hear what I just asked?"

"Yes, I heard you ask me to live with you."

"Doesn't that mean something?"

"Of course, it does. I'm just saying that life out on your own like that is hard." She let her glance fall from his. "I hear the centers can get ugly."

"They aren't that bad."

"They're dirty, and the people get in your way."

"It's only eight months."

"I'm sorry," Beatrice said. "That would just be silly when we can just wait and do it in comfort."

He pursed his lips. "The Beatrice I knew up till now would have at least considered it."

She narrowed her eyes. "Is it wrong for me to be

concerned about the place I sleep? Is it bad to think about our safety?"

He furrowed his brow again. This was wrong.

Beatrice seemed odd, standing there so passively, leaning back propped on a table's edge. Her lanky arms were set back to brace herself, the points of her shoulders pressed upward.

He'd just told her he was leaving, and she was distant and more reserved than he'd ever seen her.

"Are you okay?" he said.

"I'm fine as silk," she replied with a smile that might have been electric an hour ago.

But he didn't believe her.

He put a TS invitation up for her, and she accepted.

"Hey," he said as soon as she appeared.

From his space, he couldn't get a full read on her, but even here he could sense something was wrong. Her pattern felt different.

The flavor of challenge was gone.

Her enjoyment of the unique had been dulled.

Her flair for the dramatic was buried under a thousand different streams.

In their place she felt merely stable.

Normal.

Suddenly Maine felt the Central Inspector as a lump in his throat.

If he let himself, he knew he could imagine an artificial escort in her Think Space — maybe dressed as a security agent, standard-issue blue pants and a golden shirt with epaulets striking off the shoulders.

She'd been cut.

Stripped of the elements that made her brazen,

the things that made her who she really was. He was as sure of it as he was of the feel of air moving into and out of his lungs.

They'd been afraid of her.

The Beatrice he knew was gone.

The saddest part was that she didn't even understand what she'd lost.

The Beatrice he knew the day before would think the idea of living on his own was fabulous. She might or might not want to join him, but her impetuous nature would have spurred him on, and she would have found it fun to talk about.

But this was not the Beatrice he'd known.

"So," he said, "you wouldn't think I was doing something cool if I took out on my own?"

His stomach dropped even before she responded.

"No, Maine. That would be a bad idea."

"Come on, man!" a voice came from the middle of the room. "Kaley's ready. If you lovebirds will come along, we're going to start our discussion."

"Sure," Beatrice called out, taking Maine's hand. "Come on, Maine, let's go."

He felt her grip and returned it. But it didn't feel the same.

She stepped around him.

He followed her, clenching his jaws, trying to keep breathing, and trying to keep a tear from forming at the corner of his eye.

As he took his seat, an image flashed into his mind: Beatrice Diaz, spread in midair, her hair flying about her face, and her body crossing under a cloudless blue sky as if she would never, ever come down.

CHAPTER 13

Maine stayed on the tram past his usual stop, continuing to the outskirts of town, out in the no-man's land east into the desert. It was the deep-dark of night, 11:49 by the time he arrived at the Covina stop, the last place the city trams ran.

His brain was tired.

To avoid thinking about Beatrice during the group, he had thrown himself into Kaley's explanation of the quantum foam, and now he couldn't keep from using what he had learned as a backdrop for how he felt about Beatrice. Energy in the vacuum of space, decaying into particles, and those particles and their anti-partners meeting and annihilating within the span of such small space-time units as to be impossible to detect.

Couplings.

Pairings.

Matings.

Mutual destruction that kept an infinity of worlds going.

He couldn't help but think of Beatrice as one of those particles, exploding full of fire into his world, then, rather than being allowed to crash into him, being mined of her passion and left to fade.

He walked down Donovan Street, past card clubs and pharmaceutical lounges from which thick chords of music pounded. A housing complex lay ahead.

The night was cold now.

Maine headed for the running track here — his favorite track, his favorite place to come because they didn't light it, and so he could run in darkness, run through the night under nothing but stars.

As tired as he was now, he needed it.

He hopped the fence with ease.

He sat on a hard bench and fished his running shoes from his athletic bag, hearing Coach H's voice in the talk he gave the team before every season.

"It starts with your feet, people. Everything starts with the feet."

Then he would proceed to show the runners how to get their socks properly positioned, how to roll them over toes so they wouldn't bunch up, how to bring them down the foot, over the heel. Then how to loosen the shoe and slide it properly into place, ensuring that tightening the fasteners didn't cause creases in the socks.

"I don't want any whining or complaining about blisters," Coach H would say. *"Blisters are a sign of a poor craftsman."*

Maine went through the ritual of this process as if he were born to it.

He stripped off his jacket, then stood up.

The air was cold enough that it stung against his bare arms, and stung when he breathed it in. Anxious about followers, he glanced over his shoulder to the entry gate.

No one was there.

He pulled each foot up behind his leg to stretch his quads, then got to work on the hamstrings and his core. The arms came next. When he was done, he scanned the grounds again, finding himself still alone.

This time he laughed at himself.

"Phantom pressure," he said out loud. "You're getting paranoid."

Until he'd met Beatrice, no one else had really cared about his insane need to feel the stretch of his legs. Other than Coach H, maybe. No one else paid attention when he described the feel of his heart pumping or the scour of air scrubbing the inside of his lungs. Beatrice had, though. She'd wanted to ride along. She'd wanted to know.

She'd wanted to know more, too.

Gone deeper.

"It's dangerous to want to win so badly," his mom had told him when he'd talked about racing. "You want something like that too bad and they'll take it away from you."

But Mom was wrong, wasn't she?

If the need to win was all it took to bring the CIO down on anyone, he'd have been cut a long time ago. They didn't care about the need to win if it didn't come with something else.

Striving to win a race didn't cause people to revolt, he thought.

The CIO would care about his yearning to get away from his family, though. They would note his request, and that his parents were still able to care for him. Is that what happened to Beatrice? Had she gotten too bold in her interest in flaunting boundaries? Too independent for her own good?

The idea pissed him off.

He thought about that as he jogged down the track.

He had no choice. He wanted to win. He wanted to be the best.

But what if it were him? What if they had left Beatrice alone, and instead had taken away his need to win, his desire to compete that he felt so deeply in his bones he couldn't separate himself from it?

What would she have thought?

What would she have done?

Maybe he was too young to understand love, but all he could say for sure was that something inside him hurt, and he wished more than anything else that Beatrice was here to talk to about it.

He wanted to think she would have fought for him.

That she would have done something.

His pace picked up down the straight, then he leaned into the turn.

A tear streaked from his eye. His vision blurred, but he didn't care.

The track was dark anyway.

He was home.

His legs pumped, his feet pounded the composite surface, his arms and legs punching space like a machine. Breathing came in through the nose, out through the mouth. His muscles corrected for the torsional swing of his pelvis that he and Coach H had worked on earlier this morning.

There, in the mist of his vision and with his body pressing to use every bit of energy, he felt a remnant of Beatrice, a freewheeling essence that blazed against his mind as clear and brilliant as the stars that blazed against the nighttime sky above him.

He came out of the corner, picking up speed as he headed down the long stretch of track ahead. His timer was running, but he paid it no attention.

He was running under the stars.

As he ran, the image of Beatrice faded, and it was like the stars themselves had gone out.

When Maine woke up, late the next day, the sky was as overcast as his mood. He slid out of bed and went to the kitchen, knowing he'd overslept, but almost not caring. He'd dreamed of Beatrice and woke up feeling unhappy because of it.

His legs were tender, and the muscles of his shoulders were tight from his late run. He put his feet on the floor and cupped his hands together.

No.

He couldn't leave it sit like that. Couldn't just leave the Beatrice he knew behind.

There had to be a way.

His mother was in the kitchen, scanning a holo. She laughed at a joke.

As he went to the cabinet, his movement caught her eye.

"Hello, sleepyhead," she said.

"We're out of cereal."

"Dad probably ate the last of it."

He scowled and began gathering bread and eggs.

"Yeah," he said. They were out of butter, too, so it would have to be just jam on the toast. "But does he know where the damned requester is at?"

She paused the holo.

"We don't use that kind of language in this house."

"Yeah, well. We apparently don't know how to order food in this house, either."

Her silence drew his gaze.

"Don't give your father a hard time. He's having problems with his heart, you know."

"No, I didn't."

"How can you not know that?"

"It's not like he tells me anything." Maine would have said more, but he could feel the prickles rising in his chest, and the battle lines were already clear. His mother wouldn't have Maine calling his father lazy or listless or any one of a hundred other names that Maine would like to call him. When he was younger, Dad always had a hundred things going on, but now he was embarrassing for his lack of interest in pretty much anything.

Mostly, Maine just wanted to have breakfast and get out of the house.

"Doc bot gave him new pills," Mom said. "Says maybe he should sleep sitting up."

Maine most definitely did *not* say: *Maybe he should lose about half his weight.* Instead, he walked to the dispenser and pulled a bag of plum-orange juice, then got the pan heating and dropped bread into the toaster.

"Are you okay?" his mom said. "Looks like you're limping."

"I'm fine."

"You were running again? I thought you were with group."

"Both."

He broke eggs and dropped them in the pan. The aroma and the sound of the eggs sizzling made him even hungrier. He thought about Beatrice as he stretched his legs. He hoped his mother would drop it.

"I swear I don't see the attraction of either," she said, though. "When I was a kid, I didn't know anyone who spent time learning for no reason — and someone who said they actually wanted to run like that would have been laughed out of the neighborhood."

"Not now, Mom."

"I'm just saying. We never needed—"

He pounded his fist on the countertop.

"Really, Mom. *Not now.*"

They sat in one of those awkward silences that make it feel like the entire world had stopped rotating on its axis. His mom breathed a nasal breath, then let it out. She glanced at her holo before turning back to him.

"Is there anything I can do to help you?" she finally said.

More than anything, Maine wanted to tell his mother that yes, there was something she could do.

"I'm sorry, Mom," he said, sliding his eggs onto a plate. "No. There's nothing you can do."

The toast popped.

He spread jam over the surface, and as he ate, his mom returned to her holo.

He chewed and swallowed each bit properly and in control. That was how he was training. Control to everything. Each step in its proper spacing. Each bite with its proper purpose. When he finished breakfast, he cleaned up and put the dishes away.

He had been truthful with his mother. There wasn't anything she could do to help him save Beatrice.

There *was*, however, something he could do.

Learning Module A.12: Success Criteria (Private)

Most successful Wakers become ready to leave the medical center within three weeks, though some have taken as many as nine weeks.

Per records kept by the Central Inspector, all are living happy lives in various places around the globe and serving various functions as if they were naturally born members of society.

Wakers who take longer than nine weeks, however, are considered unsuccessful and can result in termination, with the subject's inability to learn being considered a deciding factor.

CHAPTER 14

The next day Julia escorted Bexie to his learning room once again. He wore comfortable pants and a green shirt. The chamber walls were their usual off-white.

What was different was that the chamber had a desk and chairs in it.

"Please, Mr. Montgomery," Winnie said, seated behind the desk. "Take a seat."

"After all this time together, don't you think it's time you called me Bexie?" he said as he took his seat.

The teacher leveled her fake eyes like they were a pair of handguns. They seemed harder today, the blue of the irises flaked with deeper steel.

"It is not acceptable for you to leave your quarters unaccompanied, Mr. Montgomery."

"It was a simple mistake."

"The chances of your excursion yesterday evening happening by simple mistake is less than a hundredth of one percent."

He smiled. "Okay, you've got me. I'm sorry. It's just that ... I need to do something, you know. This process is driving me loopy. Day after day after day of watching — *absorbing* — these modules. It's just not how I do things."

"And how do you do things, Mr. Montgomery?"

"I'm a hands-on guy. I try things. When they work, I learn from them."

"And when they don't work?"

"I learn from them, too," Bexie said. "In fact, failures make me learn even faster."

"That is not how things work, here."

"Why not?"

"It is our job to ensure the public is safe. If we release you too early you would cause damage."

"That makes it sound like you're a police force."

"Not exactly."

"That's an interesting question, though," Bexie said. "Who does police the public these days? That must be different, too."

"The few cases of dispute that arise are brought to the Central Inspector's Office for review."

"I would like to meet this Central Inspector."

Winnie gave a toothless smile.

"I assume you know that I've already done the transportation program you're going to run me through, right?"

"You took it as independent study two nights ago, but I need to ensure you've absorbed the material successfully."

"Look," Bexie said. "I'm really sorry about the excursion I took. But, seriously, it's true that I've taken the transportation module but it's also true that it won't help. Not really. You can give it to me again and again, but I'm not really going to get it until I get out into the real world."

"There is no other option."

"What happens if I don't ever get it, then?"

"We continue until you get it or until the contract suggests termination."

"You can't be serious."

The teacher sat motionlessly.

Bexie sat back.

"All right, then. I'll do my best. But this is wrong. I mean, how much damage can I do if you let me get on a tram in the actual city and travel around rather than sit up here in this stuffy white room?"

Winnie froze for a moment.

Then blinked her eyes in an expression of surprise.

"The Inspector's Office has agreed. They believe that experiencing the city might accelerate your comprehension. We will find a way to escort you through learning modules using the city."

"That's great!" he said, oddly perplexed. He hadn't expected such a rapid response.

"If the process is successful, it will be incorporated into future resuscitation efforts. A trial session will be configured to allow you access to the city for one day. Afterward, we will debrief the process to discover its advantages and flaws."

His hands nearly shook with the news, which surprised him but maybe shouldn't have. He hadn't realized exactly what it meant to be locked in this cage until now. Feeling this freedom made him uncomfortable in a different way. He scratched his neck and gathered his thoughts. Now was not the time to be weak.

"Can I ask for one more favor?"

"You may ask."

"Well, it's not a favor really so much as it is a suggestion."

"Go ahead."

"I'm wondering if it might be best if I could be accompanied by another human. I'm trying to relate to the world, yet all I have are Julia, you, and who knows how many other robots and whatnots. I feel a need to talk to someone like me. Someone who can really understand me."

"I am capable of linguistic and nonverbal communication in all known forms of human interaction. I am fully capable of understanding you."

"That's not what I mean."

"Then what do you mean?"

He thought about it. It was a good question.

What the hell *did* he mean?

He didn't know anyone in the world today.

Who would he be able to relate to? What did he want to know?

One name snapped to his mind, the first name he had heard upon waking, the name he had wanted to hire away from wherever the hell she was working now. She was an entrepreneur, after all. A soup stand in every store.

She would understand him.

"I want to talk to Kinji Hall," he said. "Could we have her be my escort?"

"Kinji Hall?"

"Yes. Kinji Hall. I think I could learn from her."

"All right, Mr. Montgomery. We will inquire about Ms. Hall's availability. But for now, let's focus on this module."

Bexie collected his thoughts.

"When will we know?"

"I would expect a response from Ms. Hall sometime today."

"Outstanding."

"So ... the module."

"Yes," Bexie said, standing up. "By all means, the module."

CHAPTER 15

Kinji Hall sat on the balcony of her eighth-floor flat in London and wrapped her hands around a cup of hot tea. The morning was warm, springtime just winding its way into the year. This might be the last time for the turtleneck she was wearing. This year, anyway.

She enjoyed watching the city flow. It was like a giant heart, its streets pumping people to and from everywhere so that the whole living thing that people called a city stayed alive. She liked that she could come here at any time of the day and watch it, the flow. It made her feel a connection to something she could never quite manage to describe correctly, though she never stopped trying.

She smiled at the cooing of pigeons on the roof across the alleyway.

The smells of rain and concrete wafted from below, mixing with the hydrangea plant she'd potted in the corner of the balcony.

The cup she held had been designed by an artisan

from the mountains in Chile. She had requested six of them a year ago, but one had broken when Jordan threw it off this very balcony last month. He hadn't really understood her, and their story had ended shortly thereafter. She could ask for another cup, but she liked how it felt to have a hole in the set.

Warmth from the cup felt wonderful against her fingers.

The tea's aroma was a mix of orchid and ginger, light, but gritty against the back of her throat. Its earthiness made her feel grounded.

She sipped, feeling the heat flow down to her stomach, and stared at the horizon as the sun made its way into the sky. The tea had been cultured in Lilith Station, and was one of the newer luxury items that couldn't be obtained through standard requests, yet.

Kinji had a full day planned.

She wanted to finish additions to the soup line design and send new parameters to the manufacturing printers. Requests for new installations were already arriving, so she was certain it would be made as soon as she was finished. But this moment was for getting her head on straight. She wanted to enjoy the peace of the morning.

Her pager toned inside her head.

So much for that.

Irked, Kinji twisted the corner of her lip down.

Her body chemistry altered at the sight of the avatar when she accepted the page — Tania.

She tweaked the corner of her lip twice more and

Tania's full essence appeared.

"Hey, hey-o," Kinji said.

"Hey, hey-o, girl," came Tania's reply.

They had been friends since meeting on a dance floor in Mozambique ten years ago.

"What can I do for you, Tania?" she asked.

"Well, you *could* hop on a flier and join me for dinner and a party tonight. It's been too long."

"Or you could come to London."

"I hate London."

Kinji shrugged. "Your loss."

"Fish and chips. Who wants to eat that all day?"

"Now you're just being mean."

Tania laughed. "Sorry. Just having fun."

"Seriously, babe," Kinji said. "What can I do for you? I've got to get going soon."

"You've got a request."

"A request?"

"Yeah, and a bit of a strange one at that. A Waker has asked to see you."

"A Waker?"

"You know, a person they brought back from the past. Dude froze himself or loaded himself. Whatever." Tania sent a linkpad. "Follow that for the last few reports."

"What does he want with me?"

Tania gave her a sideways glance that had naughty and mischievous slathered all over it.

"Don't you think of anything but sex, Tania?"

"Sex is art, remember?"

Yes, Kinji remembered that all too well.

"Seriously, what could a Waker possibly want with me? And why'd they contact you first?"

"I think it has to do with your soup stand design. Says he heard about it from a newsfeed and wants to talk about it. The medical center couldn't get to your node but found mine through free associations." Tania paused to fan herself in an over-the-top piece of drama. "Imagine that, little ol' me attached to important ol' you in a free association. It's enough to make a heart go pitter-patter, isn't it?"

"Sorry about that."

"No reason to be sorry, sweetie. Just make it up to me."

"I'll do that."

Kinji had locked her node to the general public a few years ago when it became obvious that most people just wanted to feed off her creativity. It had cost her because deep down she had a hard time saying no to any project that seemed interesting — and because even when people didn't know what they were talking about they often had lots of interesting ideas.

"Anyway, I thought you would be interested in this guy because, well, there aren't that many Wakers, you know? And how many of them are going to be into soup stands?"

"Not many," Kinji said. "Where is he?"

"California. San Francisco."

Tania sent the connection information.

"That's not far from Acapulco, is it?"

"Nope," Tania replied with a playful tone to her voice that made Kinji's body expand. "Not far at all."

From her balcony, Kinji scanned London. The city would be fine without her for a few days. It could still all work out, too. She could plug into the design space on the flier, and if she ran into troubles it wouldn't be the end of the world if she didn't finish the updates for another few days. Besides, the idea of a Waker being somehow interested in the soup stand idea could create interest in places she'd never considered.

An artist should always be adding, right?

That was all she knew for certain, the idea that fueled her existence — all she had ever needed.

"All right," Kinji said. "I'll check the flier schedules."

"Already done, babe."

Tania sent a fresh data stream. The next flier left London in three hours. She could make it if she packed light.

Kinji sipped more tea, and her smile grew wider as she felt its warmth in places she hadn't earlier. "You really want to see me, eh?"

"More than anything I can think of."

"All right," Kinji said, unable to hold back her smile. "I'll be there as soon as I can."

CHAPTER 16

A tone buzzed as the crowded Green Tram glided to a stop at the historic Fillmore District. Kinji Hall got out at the platform and stepped into the flow of people leaving the stop. Her bags would be delivered to her hotel room, so she'd decided to go straight to Geo-Span.

Travelling usually wore on her, but the flier from London to San Francisco had been a quick jaunt. The day was still early and shaping up to be warm and beautiful. The smell of grass and heated food from nearby cook bins wafted through the tube — which was a frosted-glass construct, open on both ends, with high arches that had been designed to ring with the hint of historic train stations.

Other travelers strode past, dressed in travel finery of processed fabrics and high hats or in simple grunge. The voices of children echoed, drawing her attention.

"I'm sorry," the father said, bending to grab one of the three boys.

"Not a problem," Kinji replied. "It's fun to see the little ones. My zone has so few!"

The father grimaced. "Two of them are just friends," he explained.

She realized the man might take her comment as criticism — to mean he'd been selfish to have three children. There were no limits, but several social circles had gotten active lately in efforts to reduce the birth rate. "I'm sorry," she said. "I didn't mean any offense."

"None taken," the man said, but he moved his kids along quickly.

Kinji's lips turned down at the corners as she watched them go. There was nothing to do for it, though. She hadn't meant to be annoying.

Moving on, she slung her sweater over her shoulder, and walked past a row of open cook pots, toward the Geo-Span Medical Center.

Her mind wandered with her gait, thinking about a motif for a line of gym clothing she was working on that would give kids something to interact with at recess periods. Historical shorts, she called them. Briefs with a brief. The idea made her smile, even as the memory of the man and his sons lingered. Perhaps he'd just had a bad day?

Her movement combined with the warmth of the sun to make her feel better. Being in San Francisco always bumped her adrenaline. It was a great city to visit, quite bohemian, filled with music that came from everywhere at once. The beat of its people pulsed rather than flowed.

Where London was merely avant-garde, San Francisco was decadent. It pushed the edge too hard for comfort.

In London Kinji's creativity came in steady streams that rolled over her like waves over an ocean beach. San Francisco, though, had this underbelly of need that was always in her face — its constant need for difference meant she felt an insistent, and persistent, demand to prove herself.

She adored visiting, though.

Passing a Canadian shop, she accepted a stick of grilled meat. "New recipe!" the vendor told her as she passed. "Thank you!" she said as she took it. She ate it as she walked but stopped and turned back to the vendor after the first taste. It was spiced with a thick flavor of maple and bourbon.

"Glorious," she called. "Well worth the exercise I'll need to burn it off!"

The thought brought her a wicked smile.

Tania was a demanding lover. With her trip to Acapulco tomorrow, perhaps it would be best to store the excess calories for a day.

The vendor waved her acceptance of the compliment.

As she was just finishing the last bits, Kinji came into view of the medical center, a tall building on the corner, with several support buildings scattered at its feet.

Waker, she thought, recalling the information she'd taken in during the flier.

Bexie Montgomery, an ancient, interested in her soup stand.

She'd seen a few clips of interviews the medical center had provided for her wherein he explained his interest in her — or at least his interest in the business aspects of her approach. She wasn't sure what to make of his explanation, but he seemed intelligent, and he was certainly attractive in a ragged kind of way. Attractive enough she could use it to ping on Tania, anyway.

This should be interesting.

The medical center had been built in the last decade, so it had a modern slant to it, a swooping roofline, external elevator shafts that wrapped around the building like vines. Its windows were a green glass that reflected the bay sunshine in a way that made her think of Jack and the Beanstalk.

She entered the medical center and took a lift to the visitor's pavilion, which was on the eighteenth floor.

The elevator car was sleek and streamlined, its progress smooth as it coiled its way up the building. She enjoyed the experience immensely, which was why it had been designed as it was. The best thing about it was the wide, majestic view of the city as it sprawled below her. Seeing it like this made her feel somehow bigger than herself, like there was something permanent about life beyond her own perception.

She scanned in when she arrived.

"You are expected, Ms. Hall," the receptionist said as Kinji's identification registered. "Your appointment is to be in room 1821. It is just down the hall."

"Thank you," she said, and walked to a room that had three nurses outside it. She smiled at them each as she walked in. Bio-ints, cloned AI hosts, or pure mechanicals aside, they were all people.

Bexie stood at the window of a receiving room. A doctor bot — which would be monitoring his reaction to the interaction — hovered in one corner, and Julia, who had escorted him to this room, was still there, standing at the doorway.

He wore what he understood might pass for a business suit in this age, an open-collared, forest green overshirt that dropped down past the hip, lined in synthetic blue trim. His slacks were black and pressed but bunched at the ankle in a way that made him feel clownish. His shoes were sandal-like platforms that wrapped around the base of his foot but left his toes and his heel open to the air. They were comfortable, though, and stable. He felt like he could run in them and not get himself hurt.

Tension growing inside him, Bexie shook his hands out.

She's late, he thought.

"Confidence is everything," he mumbled.

The view outside was fantastic. The waiting room was lower in the tower than his assigned room and revealed more of the actual streets and more of the flow of people who walked them. It was early afternoon, just past lunchtime. They had been in the room for a half hour. As far as he could tell, there'd been no change in the pattern of people at any time during the period he'd been watching. Specifically, he noted there had been no lunch rush.

The door opened, and Bexie turned.

He recognized Kinji Hall from newsfeed searches.

She entered wearing a pair of dark tights, deep burgundy, and a white tunic that flowed to midthigh. She was smaller than he'd anticipated, or rather, thinner. She walked with a stride that was more graceful than she probably thought it was.

Her smile, when she first saw him, was a brief, almost delighted upturn of one lip that gave him an image of porcelain, but softer, pliable, without the sense of brittleness that often made such people hard to deal with.

She carried no bag and hesitated only briefly as the door closed behind her.

"Mr. Montgomery," she said. "I'm very glad to meet you."

"Kinji Hall," Montgomery said as she entered, motioning her to come further into the room. He came forward from the floor-to-ceiling window, offering his hand.

She took it, though it seemed a bit formal for her tastes.

Her briefing said Wakers were walking museums, especially when it came to behavior, and that she could expect to be caught a bit off guard at times.

Montgomery's shirt was fitted close to his torso, green with a snaking design of pulsating blue wound into golden code strings to affect a flow that ran from his shoulder down his chest and past his waist on the opposite side — a design geared to accentuate a man's natural shape by making the eyes follow the flow.

Not that he needed it.

Bexie Montgomery was as beautiful in person as his holo suggested he would be. Lanky. Several centimeters taller than her, despite the heels she'd chosen for the day. His hands were long, his face pretty, his eyes comfortably dark. The whole package was one of presence.

In the corner of the room, along the far wall, a low, kidney-shaped table stood between a pair of half-couches she knew were designed by Opala, an acquaintance of hers. The table was nice, but she decided too much wing on each side made the couches feel gauche. A pot of something that smelled of an herbal coffee mix sat on the table — probably jasmine in there somewhere, but it was hard to tell with the power of coffee overriding it all.

"Can I get you a cup?" Montgomery said when he noticed her gaze.

They went to the table, and as he poured, she took a seat in the corner of one of the couches.

She noted a doctor bot that floated in the corner and the nurse standing to the side which made her decide the three outside the room were more for security than for any medical purpose.

"Thank you so much for agreeing to meet with me," the man said, handing her a cup.

"You are welcome."

She had been right about the jasmine. The combination was interesting.

"I love your accent," Montgomery said as poured his own.

"I'm glad," she replied. "I like your name. Bexie."

"Thank you," he said. "It's short for Beckingham. I think my parents wanted me to be a footballer."

She smiled because he delivered the line with a sense of amusement. "Footballer?"

"It's a sport. Or, at least it used to be?"

"I know what football is," Kinji said. "It's Beckingham that's tripping me up."

"Ah, I see." Montgomery smiled, and the couch across the table made a soft sound as he sat down. "A guy named David Beckham was a big name in the sport when I was very young. He bought an English castle and named it Beckingham."

"Well, that makes sense, then," Kinji replied.

"Anyway, enough about me and David Beckham. I think you know that I wanted to talk to you because of your soup stands."

"Yes."

Her cup clinked as she sat it on the table between them.

"You see," Montgomery said, "to make a long story short, when I came awake, I caught a newsfeed about your idea, and I thought it was brilliant."

"Thank you." Kinji blushed, despite herself.

"So brilliant that I want to buy it."

"Buy it?"

"Yes, I want to buy it. Or," he said with a warm grin, "if you prefer to hold onto a part of the net, I can build a company around it."

"I don't understand."

Montgomery leaned in.

"I want to help you," he said. "So, what do you want? How much will it cost to have you transfer the idea to me?"

She felt the weight of his gaze on her as if he was looking for a truth that went deeper than his words.

This was a moment for him. A test for her. She'd seen it before. He was playing a game.

Which design was coolest?

Which painting was best?

What kind of deal could he swing?

Kinji gave him an expression she knew would say she didn't understand — which was easy because, to be honest, she found these kinds of games quaint. She'd been briefed. She understood the concept of commerce as he described it even if she knew how outdated it was. Still, she wanted to see where he would go with it.

"Let's start here," Montgomery said. "What do you want more than anything in the world?"

Kinji picked her cup up from the table, then sat back into the couch.

The expression on Montgomery's face was open and sincere. It seemed like he really did want to help her.

She took a sip. The coffee was cooling to the point of being more gritty than hot. It made the jasmine stronger on her tongue.

"I want to create new things that are beautiful."

"And what do you need to create these beautiful things?"

"I don't understand."

But she did. Or at least she was beginning to understand some of the information she'd received from the medical center after she'd arranged the trip.

"A studio?" Montgomery said. "A design center? Tell me what you need, and I'll see what I can arrange."

Kinji slitted her eyes, finding him interesting. It was like watching a fish in an aquarium, she thought, like seeing it bounce into the walls clear as day, but unable to stop himself. It was sad in a way, though the image also made her feel better. *I can help him,* Kinji thought.

"What do you need to be more creative?" he added.

"More time, maybe," she replied.

"Yes, of course," he said with a gregarious laugh that he seemed to realize was outsized for the moment. She liked that. He wasn't a natural bore. "What else?" he said. "Do you work in a studio?"

"Sometimes."

"I can get you a bigger one."

"If I need a bigger studio, I request it and the zone committees will find me one."

"What if they say no?"

"I've never had a request turned down," she said with a grin. "Except one time when what I wanted would have made a fire hazard. The community suggested an alternative, and it turned out better."

"I see." He paused and rubbed his chin.

"Mr. Montgomery," she said. "I'm sorry, but I really don't think you understand what you're saying. I know a little about how you grew up, but we don't barter anymore. I do what I want, any time I want to do it. Like we all do. And I work with several people depending on what I want to do and what they want to do. The soup stand you are interested in, for example, was a self-configuring design. Once it was done, I put it in public space, and used collective nets to find every fashion shop in the world. The implementation followed local schedules."

"Followed?"

Kinji gave him a look like he might be crazy.
"The soup stands are already installed?"

"A few declined," she said.
Bexie stared at her, understanding that if this was true, the opportunity was lost. The doctor bot floated nearer, making him angry as it scanned him, its lights flashing an orange and blue pattern.
The rest of her words caught up to him then.
The idea that she was free to create anything she wanted at any time.
Was it possible the learning modules weren't a ruse?
Was he officially broke?
If so, did it matter?
The ideas crashed around in his brain in ways that messed up his train of thought.
"What I don't understand," Kinji said, continuing despite his confusion, "is how my soup stand is going to help you. Perhaps if you could tell me this, I could do something."
"Why did you work so hard to put soup outlets at mall stores?" he said.
She took another drink from her cup, then pulled back her lips into a reflective smile that held a hint of satisfaction.
"I did it so people could enjoy a soup while they are trying on patterns."
"But what do *you* get from it?"
"I enjoy designing new things, and I like knowing people are enjoying their soup. I get to feel the elegance of how delivery machines are built into the flow of the floor, and how the soup to arrives at the

right place at the right time.”

“That’s it?” Bexie said.

“Isn’t that enough?”

He sighed. *No*, he thought. But as he took her in, sitting forward on the couch, talking, sipping her coffee, he saw that for Kinji Hall this had been enough.

“There is an art to it, too,” she added. “I like how the systems look when I walk into a fashion center. I like how they smell.”

“Delivering soup is art?”

The smile came again. “There is art in all things if they’re done properly. Don’t you think?”

Bexie sat back, exasperated. He had pinned so many hopes on this conversation, and now they were bursting. It was true, he thought. His money was useless.

He was lost.

“I don’t get it. There is really no money in the world today?”

“I wish I could help you.”

Which was true.

There was something sincere about him. Ancient in approach, yes. But when he said he wanted to help her, he radiated sincerity.

Kinji really did want to help him.

“Perhaps I can,” she replied.

“Can what?”

“Help you.”

She saw the question in his glance.

“You asked if I could be the one to escort you through the city. So let me take you to see the soup system in action."

He laughed and his gaze shifted to the doctor bot and then the nurse.

"I would love that."

Kinji smiled. "Let's see what we can do."

CHAPTER 17

Whatever Bexie had expected, this wasn't it.

The plaza was expansive, an open-floored square that towered with eight stories of "pods" as Kinji called them (or "stores" as Bexie thought of them), and other bays on each side, with each pod existing in spaces marked off by holographic barriers and the occasional wall.

The plaza itself was littered with performers, while "shoppers" milled about watching and applauding amid their conversations. The construction included a retractable ceiling, open today to the blue sky and billowing clouds. The smell of food and perfumes drifted pod to pod, spices, and incense, and candles burning with waxy aromas. A gathering of kids strode past, eyes glazed.

"Playing a TS game," Kinji explained. "A virtual game in Think Space."

"That's incredible," he said. "I can barely talk and chew gum at the same time in Think Space."

"Your brain can adjust," she said. "Just takes a

little practice."

So much was going on all around them that he could almost forget the three security escorts flanking them. The escorts were clone-bots specialized for surveillance and control. He assumed they were linked directly back to the medical center, as well — probably — to any network the Central Inspector's Office ran. Each of the three wore casual clothes that fit into the crowd.

He wondered how many other controllers there might be in the area.

Something else he could ask Kinji if he found the right time.

Just being out, though, felt good.

Just breathing fresh air and listening to people having fun made him happy, and the smells of food made him hungry in a way that felt almost joyous.

He watched a street performer mime a magic trick that ended in a burst of flame and a puff of smoke. When the trick was done, Bexie stepped aside for a ski-boarding kid, watching him go but suddenly having an urge to try it out.

The smile on Kinji's face said she was enjoying his sense of discovery.

They passed sweet-smelling candy stands and a place that was serving some type of ground dish that smelled like cabbage.

"We can just take anything?" he said.

"It's considered proper courtesy to let the creator know if you like something they've done," Kinji replied. "But, yes, you take what you want."

They stopped for a man with a pair of neon-furred dogs to pass.

As they walked, and seeing his befuddlement, Kinji said, "This isn't how things were arranged in your time."

"Not even close," he replied. "And if we could have gotten this many people to the malls, they never would have closed."

He tried to explain the use of currency in his day.

It wasn't a system she seemed to admire.

"We learned about it when I was a kid," Kinji said at one point. "It always seemed so unfair."

He tried to explain how it wasn't unfair at all, that "it's about the energy you bring to the table," and that "you work hard, you win," but she wasn't converted.

Another stall displayed ceramics — bowls and pottery and other similar knickknacks. A holo-and-fire artist worked a circle of his own. Everywhere Bexie looked people were trying things or bickering amongst themselves. It was like nothing he'd ever seen. The vibe here was comfortable, but strange. No, the vibe here was so strange simply *because* it was so comfortable.

The people here were having fun.

A pharmaceutical outlet was built in a ring toward the middle of the space, then came a travel planning zone, which — as far as Bexie could tell — was a physical manifestation of a variety of links into Think Space, each operated by attendants talking about their favorite places.

"Do you travel a lot?" Bexie asked.

"Sure. Lots of people do."

"Where have you been?"

Kinji shrugged. "I live in London now. But I've

spent a lot of crazy days in Spain and Italy. I love the mountains in northern Italy. I get to the Americas several times a year. Chicago and Toronto a lot, and I've had probably fifteen or twenty trips to other cities here. I was in Auzzietown last year — what used to be Melbourne, I think. A full rundown would need a much longer conversation."

He scratched his head and stopped before a travel stand.

As soon as he showed interest, a holo greeter arrived before him.

"Welcome to Besters Travel Planning. You can call me Marie. How can I help you?"

"I want to go to Antarctica."

"Stop it," Kinji said.

"That sounds terribly invigorating! We have a tram leaving for Sao Paulo Central at five-thirty this evening, and a connecting flier that leaves SPC an hour later. Would you like me to let the ports know when you will arrive?"

"He's not going anywhere, Marie. I apologize for wasting your time."

Marie laughed. "No reason to apologize. I love having browsers. The last time I was in Antarctica the penguins were amazing."

Kinji pulled him away and the holo disappeared.

"Why did you do that?"

"I wanted to know what would happen. No one pays for my flight if I go, right?"

She pulled him harder by the elbow, while he looked over his shoulder to take in a holo of a surfer outside of Sydney somewhere. "Maybe you try that when they've let you out of the memory palace, eh?"

"Memory palace," he said. "I like that."

She made a goofy expression with her eyes wide.

His sigh was heavier and probably sounded more miserable than he intended, but he suddenly found himself unable to think about anything other than surfing with Kinji. When she pulled him away, the pressure she put on his arm felt good, and the smile in her voice was quite lovely. Yes, she was quite lovely, but that was only part of his impression of her. The rest was something he couldn't explain but was tied up in the fact that she was even willing to come here in the first place.

Technically, merely agreeing to accompany him outside was probably taking a risk — security escorts or not. The medical center seemed intent on keeping him under surveillance. If something happened, he wondered what kind of shit she might find herself in.

"I've never gone surfing," he said as Kinji led him through the crowd.

"Maybe this summer," she replied.

As they left the travel zone, Bexie felt two of his escorts draw closer, a realization that made him tense up, which, in turn, made him realize how good he'd been feeling until then — exactly how good it felt to be outside now and to walk in this open space full of energetic people engaging in what, to his eyes, suddenly did seem like a utopian free-for-all where everyone got whatever they wanted. After building his entire life around consumerism, this felt so weird he could hardly get his brain around it, but at the same time, being here was as close to his "home ground" as he had felt since the moment he'd become Awake. The act of shopping as safari struck him. The hunt for the right thing at the right time was ingrained in what it meant to be a human being, after all. What a person does defines that person, and while his own culture revolved around work, this one had grown around something else instead.

Contribution.

Expression.

Enjoying who you were.

Whatever it was, this act of hunting what you enjoyed or what you needed was what made life what it was.

The fact that these things were shared among each other was something he had to get used to, but thought he liked.

Glancing at the nearest escort, however, brought him back to Earth. He didn't like the scrutiny.

Finally, they entered a fashion pod — one which would be using Kinji's system. It was an actual room in the outer edge of the plaza's ground floor, a large section of the northernmost wall of "shops" with a collection of platforms configured around the floorplan, most of which had customers standing on them.

"Simulators," Bexie mumbled as she took his hand and led him through the crowd.

"Exactly," Kinji said, pointing to the platform. "You get to enjoy trying things on here, and if you like something, it will be requested and delivered."

"No money, of course?" he quipped.

Her eyes became shaded with fake anger, and she shook her head sullenly while mouthing a silent "no."

A moment later they came to one of the simulators.

A young woman stood on the platform wearing a jumpsuit with holes cut from the midriff and the knees. The image of a panther's head was designed into the right shoulder, its eyes gleaming green.

A friend leaned over and laughed at her, hand cupped over her mouth. "You should wear that to Junu's!" she yelled.

The model rolled her eyes and paged to the next design.

"Do you design clothes?" Bexie asked.

Kinji nodded. "Not often, but it's fun sometimes."

They left that platform and went to an alcove off the main area that was labeled as "Hanshu's" — clearly an upscale boutique. They passed a collection of physical scarves and lingerie hung on sections that marked the circumference of the space, and continued through displays that focused on midcalf coats and dresses that seemed fine enough to be made of air.

"What do you think of these, Bexie?" she asked, running her fingers over a scarf.

"Reminds me of Miyake — Japanese haute couture," he replied.

"I love that period," she said.

The expression on her face said she knew what he was talking about.

"Maybe some Russian, too," Bexie added, letting his mind adjust to the idea of Miyake being *that period*. "From the nineteen fifties, anyway. Russian fashion changes as often as its politics." He couldn't remember where that line originated, but it hung in his memory.

"Interesting," Kinji said. "This designer has strong Russian lines in her heritage."

They stopped at a rounded simulation platform with a man and a woman modeling together.

"Try to pull my TS here," Kinji said. "You'll get a better fidelity."

"How do I do that?" he said.

"Concentrate. Feel for the closest one. Until you get a little more used to it, you might feel two or three. But usually you can figure out the right one."

He tried and got the line of a candy maker.

He tried again and found himself seeing things from both her viewpoint and his. It was so disorienting at first that he had to grab Kinji's bicep to keep from falling over, but after a moment, his mind seemed to figure it out. Focusing mostly on Kinji's experience, he watched.

"Let's try the first," the woman said.

Her original clothes — a sleeveless top and a black skirt with silvered hose — dissolved into a flowing golden gown that luminesced with her movement. She was not a particularly noticeable woman, but Bexie had to admit she would be hard to miss in that dress.

"Darker eyes," the man said.

The woman's eyes grew into coaled circles that made the blue of her eyes stand out.

"Make the dress titanium rather than gold?" she asked.

"Amazing!" Kinji said from afar. "But darken the detail."

The dress adjusted to those specifications.

"Red lips," the woman added. "Cherry."

"Darker," Bexie said. "A mixture of wild cherry and raspberry."

The woman giggled.

"It's smashing," she said. "Don't you think, honey?"

"It is."

"Will Jinny think so, too?"

"Jinny will love anything you put on, Suze." His expression formed into a lighthearted leer. "Or take off, for that matter."

"Why, yes," the woman said, fanning herself, and using the singsong tone of a diva. "She will, won't she?"

Kinji stepped away, Bexie following, the pair leaving the shoppers alone.

"We'll make a designer out of you, yet, Mr. Montgomery."

The feel that came through her TS as he dropped it was one of respect.

"I do my best. Are you going to show me your soup stand?"

"Yes," Kinji said. "But first—" she pointed to an empty platform. "Get up there and show me some fashion."

Bexie gave a guffaw. "You've got to be kidding."

Kinji got wide eyes again and shook her head to the negative.

"I'm not a model," he argued.

He sensed something specific to that head shake, something of a challenge in her gaze. Was Kinji Hall testing him?

"Don't be shy, now," she said. "You want to know

how this shit works — get up there and show me some fashion.”

He looked at people milling about, smiling and having a good enough time. Why not?

The pathway up was three steps. He took them briskly.

The platform was maybe three meters across, and ringed at the edge with something that glittered darkly. It was a projection ring, he figured. A key element of a holo simulator.

“What do I do?”

“Stand back,” Kinji said, waving a throng of shoppers away. “The first one’s mine!” Then she stepped back and gave a contemplative scan as she assessed his physique.

“Show me a Trava,” she called out. “Black top, something blue as a pant.” She smiled savagely. “And dragon boots.”

The ring lit up, and he saw himself in a suit. Lifting his feet, he found the boots came to his knees and had laces up the side. The leatherwork of each boot was etched with the body of a dragon — the left having the dragon’s head with its toothy maw at the toes, the right with the tail looping down the foot and the head nestled on the inside of the knee.

“Very sharp,” he said.

“Indeed,” Kinji replied. “Turn around, let me see the back.”

He turned, and felt the way the suit fit, how the fabric moved against his body.

Kinji gave a clicking sound that he took as appreciation. “Okay,” she said. “Now let’s see a Mackenzie Sheffer suit with a pair of screens.”

The holo changed, and Bexie was wearing something different. He didn't like it as well, though the "screens" were apparently a set of squared eyeglasses of multiple hues. He noticed two shoppers had stopped and were watching.

"Make it more to the red," one of them said, and Bexie's entire outfit changed from a yellow base to a shade of burnt orange. The cuffs were black, then blue, then a darker orange.

"Nice," Kinji said to the man. "But I think he needs something stronger at the shoulder, don't you?"

The man shrugged. "If you like that in a man."

She scowled and raised her eyebrow.

One shoulder of Bexie's outfit darkened, and he felt a pad grow that added a sharper edge to his profile.

"Turn that ass around!" another spectator said.

Bexie stood there, then turned and did something awkward that approached a shimmy.

Another whoop came from the gathering, this one tinged in sarcasm.

"That is *not* going to get the job done," Kinji yelled above the din, rotating her finger in the air to indicate he should move even more. "Let yourself go up there, baby! Have some fun! Turn your ass around and do your century proud!"

The crowd voiced approval for the idea.

This was a different situation, but he'd dealt with groups in the past.

His smile was awkward, but he dug down into the performer in him, steeled himself, and threw himself into the role.

He took a superhero pose, legs spread comfortably, chest extended, hands balled at the waist. People gathered around, and light flashed. Cheers rose. It reminded him of paparazzi, but without the aggressiveness.

Raised on the platform, he had a good view of the shop's layout.

He saw niches he hadn't seen before — rooms and nooks where, as the idea struck more firmly, maybe he could hide if he could slip away.

He saw how people flowed through the place, *optimal paths* consultants used to call them in the old days. Paths that most shoppers took, which then commanded premium advertisement rates.

He took a serene pose and, while the audience tweaked the fit of his shirt, took notice of where the three security escorts were — one to each side of the platform, the third wandering in the free flow of patrons around the floor. He could almost hear them chattering about him across unseen networks. Could he lose them?

He took another pose, scanning for other monitors. They had to be out there, didn't they? Then another pose, more outrageous than the last.

Kinji applauded along with the rest, her long, graceful fingers almost wrapping around her hands with each clap.

"You're a natural," she said.

Okay," he finally said. "It's time for someone else to get up here."

"Only after you choose which ones you want," Kinji said.

"Awesome," he said, nearly giggling. "I don't

know. Which did you like best?"

"Maybe the blue Messer, and a pair of thin slacks."

"Done."

"And the dragon boots, of course."

Bexie grinned. The boots were ludicrous, but he wasn't going to spoil her fun, and screw it, they'd been a blast to show off in. "*And* the dragon boots. So, how do I take it all to my palatial estate?"

"Just tell Think Space this is the outfit you want."

He nodded. "I'll take this," he said, finding an open channel.

"*Where should it be delivered?*" Think Space's voice was neutral.

He didn't have anywhere else to suggest, so he said, "How about the memory palace!"

"*I don't have record of such a place,*" the voice said.

"Of course not," Bexie replied. "How could you?"

Kinji gave the wry expression he was hoping for.

"The Geo-Span Medical Center," he finally said. "Mark it for Beckingham Montgomery."

This would work better anyway, he thought. If nothing else it would send the message that he was coming back, but Bexie was certain of one thing and one thing only. If he could manage it, he was not going back into that prison again. And if he did have to go back, he was getting the hell out of Dodge as soon as possible.

"*Your delivery will be made by the end of the day.*"

CHAPTER 18

Yes, Kinji decided, there was something to Bexie Montgomery.

Along with the rest of the crowd, Kinji applauded again as he came off the stage. She'd seen performance highs before, but Bexie's was an intense wave of giddiness that spooled together to put him on the edge of control. A man shoulder-bumped him, and Bexie burst into laughter. An androgynous fan offered him half a sandwich and a trip into a quiet nook, which made him blush and made Kinji take more control.

"Looks like you had fun."

"It beat the hell out of being locked up in the medical ward."

"Well, we'll have to break you out more often."

"Don't say it if you don't mean it."

Kinji gave him a sideways glance that was half double take.

His voice had been lighthearted, but there had been another layer to it, and the intensity of his glance made her step back a notch. Not everyone would have seen it, but Kinji noticed then how he scanned the area like he was looking for a weakness or a path, and she saw how he constantly cycled through the crowd to note exactly where the medical center's escorts were.

Tania, for example, would have plowed right along, oblivious even to the comment.

But Kinji felt a feral hint of despair, or was it hope, in his comment, just a touch, a spice, like the jasmine that had been in her coffee earlier in the day.

Indeed, Bexie Montgomery was even more interesting than she had considered possible. For a moment, she wondered if the CIO would let her take him to Acapulco tonight, then dropped the idea. But another came in its place, one she wasn't so sure about.

If she was right, Bexie Montgomery was going to bolt. Maybe not now, but soon.

Could she help him?

Or, rather, was she willing to take that kind of chance?

If he was successful and the CIO found her helping him it could get ugly.

"So," Bexie said, "are we ever going to get to see how your soup stand works or is this really just you deciding you wanted to take a joyride with a dinosaur?"

"Well, I do like dinosaurs, but let's do it," she replied.

She stepped past a group of people who were now admiring another young woman modeling rain gear.

After a short walk, Kinji and Bexie arrived at a pear-shaped station lined with seats, mostly full of people spooning soups of various kinds, mostly chatting together, but two clearly linked into something in Think Space. A hole in the middle of the thick part of the station was large enough that equipment could be seen to run underneath the stand.

"Link into my feed," she said, sending him an invitation.

This was the moment, she thought, the test.

While she waited for his connection, she slipped a part of her conscious thought even deeper into her space than others would know about. Something others knew as Free Think, but that she called her True Space, a place overlooked, a place she owned and no one else could touch. If Bexie turned out to be the person Kinji was beginning to think he was, she would need to be in True Space to create a new link for him.

She sat, waiting.

There was an awkward pause, then his essence came in so hard it was almost disorienting.

Bexie felt the invitation as deep red flash in the back of his mind, much bolder than the last time.

Expecting a simple transfer, he latched onto it.

This time, though, the connection was like plunging his face into a sink full of water. One moment he was fine, the next his breath was taken away. His vision swam, and sound condensed to a single pop.

Then he blinked and he was fine.

"You've never ridden a wire down this deep, have

you?" Kinji said through their connection. He noted the tips of her fingers were pressed against the countertop as if to keep her stable.

He blushed. "You could tell?" he said out loud.

She laughed.

"Follow me along here," she sent him.

This deep, he liked how her voice felt, but before he could luxuriate in its calmness, she was moving on, showing him the graceful flow of something that was part tabletop and part sculpture, but also an elegantly conceived service center.

Design documents came to his view as he felt her fingers roll over the surface.

It was a strange sensation, operating in the physical world and being in Think Space at the same time.

"It's wonderful," he said through his link, though he wasn't sure if he was commenting on the soup stand or simply on being able to feel the softness of her hands. With time to assess, the connection she'd given him was strong, different from his own. The sensation of her hands, for example, was delicate. He felt their warmth against his. If he concentrated hard enough, he thought he could feel the soft hairs on the back of them.

Was he imagining it?

She continued around the station.

The system was a smooth extension of the floor, its pedestal rising with a flow that felt like something made of evolutionary erosion rather than built by a human's hand. The base was a simple black composite twined with a rose plant that ran its height to warp over the edge of the counter. The stools around it were soft and elevated. On one side, for people who wanted to loiter, was a pair of beige couches embroidered with a rose pattern that matched the station's accent.

"Feels ... like you just need to have a seat, doesn't it?" he said.

"I'm glad you like it," Kinji said, a sense of appreciation in her tone. "The materials are stored in a kitchen component under the floor. See how it works?"

The floor disappeared from his view, and now the lower portions of the delivery mechanism were visible — inventory bin, matter converters, mixing stations, and the heating unit.

He watched raw materials flow into the mixer, water get added, and each individual bowl of soup heated to the proper specification. The final product was poured into a holding compartment and moved along a conveyor to the station that had made the order, where it was presented to the requestor in a bowl that was configurable per each type of soup.

Growing more comfortable being in her link, he felt the movement of her hand as she operated hidden compartments to present a menu for people to make requests from, and then showed him dispensers for serving the soup.

"You present the soups in different bowls?"

"Of course," Kinji replied. "Porcelain for a broth, compound for a soup, stoneware for a stew."

"Well done," Bexie said.

He pointed to the gap between a sofa and a side table.

"What if you extended the table out to the edges

of the sofas, then deliver the soup to their side tray?"

"That would make sense, too," Kinji said, her voice notching up a bit. "I like it. That way the clients wouldn't need to turn away from each other to enjoy their soup. I'll put it in a design note for the next installation."

"Thanks."

"I'm thinking of making the center gap display rose bushes as if they are waving in the wind," she said.

"I like that," Bexie replied.

They were both silent for some time, then. Through Think Space, Bexie examined the system further, then took in the crowd that gathered around in the physical. They were just people, here, chatting and laughing, or relaxing. They were just having soup.

The farther he was into Kinji's Think Space, the more comfortable he felt.

No. Comfortable was the wrong word. Intimate was better. Or exposed.

Not in a physical way, though. Not intimate as a sexual thing, or exposed as in vulnerable, but closer and safer, like they were simply alone in the most intense way it was possible to be alone.

"Can they hear us here?"

Kinji's face betrayed a moment's uncertainty.

"Yes," she said. "We are all modified to be born with TS links inside our head, and the connections grow deeper in our first years so that they are a part of us. They are all we ever know, so we grow comfortable with them, but if the Central

Inspector's Office is watching, it can see everything about all the people you see here."

Bexie did his best to hide his disappointment, but he wasn't dumb enough to kid himself that he hadn't failed miserably.

Kinji touched the back of his hand.

"I'm not sure about you, though."

"What do you mean?"

Her expression was guarded, but it also registered an uncertainty of some kind. A question, maybe, or a warning. He wasn't sure what message she was sending, but for a moment he felt something dangerous.

"You mean ..."

He glanced to the nearest escort, taking in its unlined face. As he watched, the security guard pursed his lips in a way that was very human.

Could the escorts sense him? Could they see through his eyes? Could they feel the touch of Kinji's hand on him? That was what Kinji was implying, wasn't she? She wasn't sure if Bexie was connected yet. And if he wasn't connected, then...

He reached for the escort through TS.

The escort didn't respond.

Bexie felt his eyes grow wide. Did that mean they couldn't feel him? Couldn't trace him like they traced others?

Was that why they'd sent three escorts rather than just one? Why, perhaps, he'd been able to follow Julia down the hallway without being sensed or followed? If they could have known where he was during his escape, they would have stopped him, but he'd only been caught by Julia herself, and, even then, only by happenstance. If he'd gotten away, could he have run forever?

The escorts were here specifically because they couldn't track him.

"There are some people, very few in number, who have no links," Kinji said in an offhand way.

"Really," Bexie said.

"They consider themselves rebels," she continued, speaking to him as if she were merely passing conversation. But Bexie felt more going on under the surface. Kinji Hall's voice was perfectly expressionless. "They live outside, you know? And..." She hesitated in a way that seemed important. "I'm also aware of people who can build a TS wall so tight not even the CIO can get in."

"I see."

And he did.

Or at least he was starting to.

"Does it go the other way? Can anyone talk to the Central Inspector?"

Her expression mixed bemusement with sarcasm, and her gaze scanned the area around them in a way that amped his already high sense of unease.

"Maybe that's a topic for another time."

"That's a cop-out."

"I don't understand."

"You're being evasive," he said.

She nodded. "Yes, I am."

He prodded her with a raised eyebrow.

"Some people say there's a way."

"To get to the CIO?"

"Yes. I've heard rumors. But that's all. If there's really a way, I don't know it."

"How about tracking?" he asked, recalling the security files his businesses kept. "Do they keep logs of what they find?"

"Some," Kinji replied. "I can't say for sure how in depth they are, though. No one really knows."

Bexie considered the information he'd just gotten dumped on him.

Thought about how certain things worked.

Or maybe didn't.

Jesus, this place was a mess, wasn't it? Free as free could be in one way, but uncomfortably dystopian in several others. The whole thing made the back of his neck itch. Now more than ever, he wanted to figure out who he was in this new world. And he wanted to spend time with people like Kinji. He wanted to be free — or at least out from under the eyes of the medical center. Wanted to meet these rebels she spoke of.

Another quick scan of the area convinced him he could pull it off.

He may not understand the world at large today but he understood a few things about doing business, and the first rule of doing business was that you could gain a lot of distance if you got people focusing on one thing while you were really doing something else.

Something about Kinji's comments piqued his attention, something in the way her voice rose made him think there was more to her than met the eye and made him think about his *second* rule of doing business — that life got easier when you were a monopoly.

That's what the Waker process was, after all: The

excessive studying, the logging his Think Space into their modules. He'd been looking at his learning modules as indoctrination, which, while true, was only part of their reason to exist. Bexie and the rest of the Wakers had not been born during the time of Think Space. Their DNA was "pure."

The truth of the matter is that he'd never had to learn anything more than a few simple basics: how to use Think Space, how to request things, a few bits of etiquette, and maybe how to find places to sleep. Food was free for the asking, after all. Clothes, too. It was valuable to have a sense of the public, but mostly that was a learned practice, anyway.

But the training *was* serving a purpose.

Brainwashing.

Or, if not brainwashing, at least control.

Was there a difference?

This whole process was designed to buy time for their technology to eat its way through his mind — as it did through the heads of every child born over the past hundred and fifty years.

The idea struck him so hard that Kinji felt his reaction.

She grabbed his hand and stared hard into his eyes.

Slowly, she sketched a pattern on his arm with the fingers of her other hand. It was writing, he realized. She kept her eyes riveted on his. He felt his breath quicken, and adrenaline flooded his brain.

We have a place that is ours, she wrote. *Look for the blue in your Think Space.*

Then she let go, and her gaze dropped.

He glanced at his escorts. They shifted feet but

did not appear to react. He stared back at her, feeling like time had stopped in both places at once.

They couldn't feel him.

He felt Kinji's gaze.

"So," Bexie said to her in the physical, rattled but not obviously so. "How do you submit a final design?"

"It's simple," she said, pushing a common channel to him and adding a comment that noted five locations that had already requested the system. While he watched, she marked the change Bexie had suggested, and put a notice in several other bins, then released it. "That lets the others know the design is available. Planners at any site can simulate it for safety and determine if unintended consequences might occur. If they like it, they will approve, and request the design be made."

"By robots, right?"

"Sure. Autonomic entities, anyway." She joked, "The term *robot* is so twenty-first century."

"And robots even make the robots."

"Autonomic entities make…"

"Yes, yes." He cringed, trying to split his thought processes to assess Kinji's command to look for blue in his Think Space at the same time as they held this conversation. "And who does the simulation of Kinji Hall's latest design?"

"Anyone can, really. But if nothing else, there's always a wing element of the Central Inspector's Office."

"And where is that? Can we talk to them?"

"Never tried. Results of the simulation get

released in a day or two. It just happens."

Bexie nodded.

His searching found nothing blue, though, which gave him a sense of panic because the urgency in Kinji's expression said more was going on here than met the eye. He had to be missing something but had no way to ask without arousing suspicion.

He stood and watched a group on the platform. Two were up there now, but he realized that it wasn't really them. Instead, they were a projection of a couple who sat on the sofa.

"You can do that?" The words slipped out of his mouth before he thought to hold them back. He watched the couple, though, and saw they were using the process to see themselves in whatever fashions they were interested in — helpful, especially if you didn't have a group of people to tell you what was working for you or not.

"Sure," Kinji replied.

They went back to the platform. "Join my TS again. I'll show you."

He followed her invitation.

"Add yourself to the stream for this location, and project yourself."

An image of Kinji appeared on the stage. He saw how she did it, and a moment later, Bexie joined her.

Kinji left to sit on the sofa again, but rather than follow this time, Bexie jumped onstage with his holo double. "This is freaking insane," he said. "Now there's two of me."

"Yes," she said. "We can't keep it up forever, though. It takes a lot of energy."

He passed a hand through his double. It was an opaque image. Yes, he thought. Opaque. Like the boxer who had nearly gutted him with a punch.

"Very fresh," he said, laughing aloud, and noting the escorts were watching closely. He held his hand out to his double's hand, pressing his thoughts into it, pressing his hand into the double's hand, feeling its counter pressure as he gave it more attention. And, at the same time, understanding something else. The projection worked on a public channel — he could see the other's projections because they were casting into his TS, and others could see his projection because he was casting into theirs.

He turned to his double and made him dance.

Taking great joy, he turned his own body around.

"I'm dancing with myself!" He laughed, turning a strange step into something that might be called a do-si-do.

People gathered around him, and the stage became his.

A few minutes later, Bexie came back to the sofa where Kinji had returned, perspiration gleaming on his sternum. The double was gone, and others were already modeling themselves.

"Are you ready to go back?" Kinji asked.

"In a moment," Bexie said still gasping for breath. "Just a minute."

Kinji stared slack-jawed, staying in her True Space as best she could.

Until the moment Bexie had made the swap, she hadn't known for sure if he could do it. But she'd seen that slick moment — that brilliant piece of art within itself — when Bexie Montgomery had literally changed places with his double, projecting himself into TS so fully that his double responded to touch.

Until that moment, she could have backed out, could have stolen back into Bexie Montgomery's TS and disassembled the construct she had left behind earlier. In that moment, though, she made her final decision about this strange man from the past.

For all his outdated ideas, he was a good man at heart.

At least it seemed that way to her.

He had every right to live.

So, when he cast his hologram to sit next to her she played it straight. And when it was asking to wait a moment so it could catch its breath she let it happen, knowing the real Bexie Montgomery needed to find a place to be alone, a place to stay away from prying eyes and ears and sensors — knowing how unlikely it was he'd succeed, but knowing he needed his chance.

Then, finally, she rose and took his hand, which was so firm it impressed her. Even better, she knew, it gave her a free pass. She'd been duped, she'd be able to say, and as long as they didn't pry *too* deeply, as long as they didn't presume *too* much, she could prove it.

Kinji led him away, security falling in step beside them.

As they got a dozen or more steps away from the stage, Bexie disappeared, just fell away as if he had never been there in the first place, as if he were a hologram that had gotten too far away from its source — which is exactly what it was.

The escorts reacted immediately.

One grabbed Kinji by the wrist, the other shut down barriers to the shop. The action registered on every person in the mall, and they each drew up sharply. The third escort reported the situation, and in only a few seconds more security arrived — clone controllers, police bots, and other mechanical devices focused their attention on the area.

But it didn't matter.

Bexie Montgomery had escaped.

CHAPTER 19

Security scanned the area for several minutes, finding nothing, before calling in the Global Police. They, too, were unable to find Bexie Montgomery.

Kinji was actually surprised at this, though maybe she shouldn't have been.

She had given him such a small entryway into the fold that she was certain he would miss it, and the time to flee had not been extensive. But Bexie Montgomery was apparently more adroit at picking up patterns than might first appear, and, somehow, he'd gotten out.

It only served to make her more certain of her decision.

They took her to the Zone 98 Central Inspector's Office, where she waited for an inspector to arrive. The room they kept her in was stark — which made sense.

She felt a chill.

The place's lack of odor added to its edge, and the hard chair they gave her was a weapon all by itself.

There was no safety here, no place to hide.

The inspector entered, an easily identifiable autonomic entity constructed of clone material of a masculine form, dressed in regimented blue. It strode briskly to the table to take a seat.

"May I get you a tea?" the inspector asked.

"No, thank you."

"I need to ask you why you came to San Francisco."

"Why do you have to ask that? You already have my submission."

"I need to hear it from you, or are you just avoiding the question?"

"I can't avoid answering what I've already answered," she said. "Why I am being treated as a prisoner?"

"This is standard procedure for such an outbreak."

"I see."

"You are an artist?"

"Yes."

"That is an interesting label."

"How so?"

"There are not a lot of people who claim such."

Kinji shrugged. "I can't help it."

"What do you mean?"

"Artists don't decide to be artists. We just are. I can't help that I see ideas everywhere."

The inspector made a dismissive expression that started with his lips and flowed up to his eyes.

Kinji straightened, this time perhaps with a bit more defiance.

The inspector's expression was more grimace

than smile.

"I'm sure we can agree there is no art here, eh, Ms. Kinji Hall."

"Quite the contrary."

"No?"

"This inquiry itself, for example," Kinji said. "There is a simple cycle that some might call a ritual, which is arguably one of the most disciplined of all arts. There is a pulse to it, right? A feel to it? A well-done interrogation builds on itself, doesn't it? And it grows on its own, I suppose. Doesn't it? Sometimes winding up in places that are totally different than what had seemed preordained only moments before?"

Kinji hesitated only a beat.

"So, yes, inspector, there is a great deal of art here in this room."

The inspector seemed to pause.

"What do you know of Mr. Montgomery's escape?"

"Was Mr. Montgomery a prisoner?"

"How is that an answer?"

"It could not be an escape unless he were escaping from something. Your question implies he was a prisoner."

"He was being held under medical quarantine."

"The medical center gave me no reason to believe he was contagious, so I had no cause to consider him dangerous in that way, or even to think he would run away, hence I was not paying attention to him in that fashion."

"So, you did not aide him?"

"No," she replied.

She was sure the inspector would already have processed the scan of her experience at the shop. The question at hand was whether she was as correct as she thought she was. If her safe block wasn't truly safe, she was in trouble. Otherwise, she should be fine.

"You saw him leave, though."

"I saw him step off the platform, and I knew the version of him that sat beside me was the hologram."

"And you did nothing to point that out?"

"I thought he was playing a game. We've all done it at some time or another. He was clearly having fun learning how to use projection. I mean, it's fun to try to pass off your double to your friends. I was surprised no one else noticed."

"And you have no idea why he left?"

She shrugged. "Perhaps he was afraid of you."

"He was treated to the most comfortable environment."

"Maybe he was just bored."

"Did he say anything to you that would make you say that?"

"It was clear he was anticipating his release, but beyond that I couldn't say." She pressed her hands into the armrests of the chair. "I can understand that. I think it's fair to say we can both agree that freedom is what makes life worth living."

"Of course, it is, Ms. Hall," the inspector said with a more comfortable smile. "And we wouldn't want to have to take that away from you."

The length of silence grew uncomfortable.

"Do you have any other questions?"

"Just one." The inspector leaned over the table. Kinji waited.

"Do you have any idea where Bexie Montgomery is right now?"

Kinji's smile was deep and full of relief. For once she could say something with the full force of the truth behind it.

"No, inspector. I have no idea where Bexie Montgomery went."

CHAPTER 20

Bexie's heart pounded as he slipped from the platform. He took a step, then hunched to his belly to snake along close to the floor, continuing until he was behind a fully opaque billboard that was rotating ads every few seconds.

Glancing, he saw his escorts hadn't responded.

He felt suddenly exposed, though.

He'd projected his hologram, of course, and at the same time he'd projected an aura of nothing around himself. Made himself essentially invisible. But it was hard to do, and now that he didn't have the misdirection of his second around him, he gave it up completely.

He expected an army of robots to come streaming out of secret openings in the walls at any moment.

Stop it, he thought. *There's no time for this kind of crap.*

How long did he have before someone — or something — would catch on?

Kinji would help him, but the time she could give

him was short.

He used a clothes rack and other displays to slip further into the "store." He'd seen an exit in the back corner. The path there felt every bit a no-man's land, but with some luck he could make it.

People strolled past. He saw their shoes and leggings beneath the rack.

With the Central Inspector's Office linked into every brain in the world but his, each one of these people was a mobile security camera.

He needed to alter himself, and he needed to do his best to avoid contact.

A hat stand stood nearby. He grabbed a wide-brimmed model and pushed it down on his head. *Stylish, Montgomery.*

Picking a moment, he walked briskly until he came to a nook that housed a small apothecary whose owner was engaged in schooling a customer on chemical compositions. He juked left, then right, then nearly ran into a man who had left a pastry dispensary. He ducked his head, and apologized, moving immediately on and brushing sugary residue from his shoulder.

A man's coat lay over a seat. Dark leather with a tint toward indigo.

He shouldered it on as he continued toward a rear exit.

The coat was light despite its materials, with a serrated collar.

He found a pair of sunglasses in one pocket, and put them on as he walked, hoping his movement was calm and easy.

Probably didn't make a difference, but he would

do anything that might put any computer mapping algorithms off. The glasses darkened his view, which he wasn't sure he liked, but if it made him more difficult for face assessors to identify, then it would be worth it.

Bexie gathered up his wits and collected the shell of confidence that had served him so well for so many years.

Just like pulling down a major deal, he told himself.

Focus.

Stick to what's important now.

He merged into the press of people, taking only one glance behind to check for tails but finding none.

The exit was so close.

Each step came with agonizing slowness.

He really wanted to run.

The door.

There.

He pushed, hoping it wasn't locked.

Then he was outside in the sunshine of late afternoon, into the breeze that smelled of concrete and of salt.

And into a stream of humanity. Jesus. He'd seen it from his room above the skyline, and he'd understood that these people were not workers, that a hundred percent of their day was spent in some form of leisure activity, socializing, or entertainment. But seeing it from a couple hundred meters away and being there were two different things.

The city was packed.

He pulled the brim of his hat down against the sunshine, and turned right without hesitation, slipped behind a row of trams, then took another right and walked through a wide plaza — an open patch of sidewalk lined with food stations of all types.

Keeping his head down, he kept moving.

Ahead of him, a woman spoke about her boyfriend and another responded with pithy advice about keeping a dog.

Two men and a woman argued about a geo-play, which Bexie didn't fully understand but realized had something to do with the players being in remotely separate locations, but still playing off each other.

Voices jumbled. The sound of footsteps rumbled.

He focused on those, tried to decide if he heard footsteps behind him or ahead for that matter. A man walking beside him seemed to be studying Bexie's face. Bexie turned to look the other way, seeing a sequence of cameras and sensors lining the streets.

Christ, he thought.

He thought about eating but wondered if the Central Inspector's Office would have them wired. Would a Chicago dog be the bane of his existence?

A tram was waiting at the next station — the car painted red and advertised as an "old San Francisco Trolly!" It was a little larger than an old-style bus but open to the air and ringed with rails to keep riders — who were already crammed in — from falling out.

He needed distance, and he needed it now. Could he just step on?

Bexie grabbed a rail and swung onto the platform just as it lurched away.

A woman elbowed him for space. "What the hell are you doing?"

"Sorry," he muttered as he edged away, gripping the rail for dear life.

One of the learning modules had explained the use of high-temperature superconductors in creating this smooth ride, but he was still unprepared for the sensation of gliding through the air without any sound other than the conversations of fellow riders. He felt the heat of their bodies, and the pressure of their closeness.

The buzz and the feeling of motion combined to calm him down.

Raising the brim of his hat, he glanced up the road.

With his memory of San Francisco over three hundred years behind him, his concept of the city's layout was useless. But he was pretty sure he was in the southern regions of what he knew as Bernal Heights.

He needed a next step. A place to run.

As the tram glided over the street, Bexie saw a furious stream of construction happening everywhere.

Automated cranes, and crushing machines, and tumblers mixing material, and bot units scaling the sides of buildings to lay beams in their cross-slots a couple hundred meters in the air.

The image reminded him of grainy black-and-white photos taken in the days of the first industrial revolution of men sitting on these beams hovering above the surface of the earth hundreds of meters below, eating their lunches as if it were nothing.

He wondered what those men would say if they could see this.

A buzz seemed to come over the tram.

People scanned the area.

"Is he running?" a woman said.

In the distance he thought he saw a collection of security bots gathering.

A woman shouldered into him.

"Hey!" She turned, grabbed a fistful of his collar and nearly lifted him up to his toes. "What are you doing there, shoving up against me?"

Bexie glanced at the woman standing beside her.

"And now you're looking at my girl, too?"

"I'm sorry, miss."

The woman stared at him, her eyes constricting to a pair of points. He could almost hear the click of a camera and sense the packets of information coalescing inside the woman's head and racing up to where the CIO would put it all together.

He panicked, then.

Without thinking, Bexie grabbed a rail and leaped over it.

The tram was still traveling, and he tumbled to the ground, rolling to break his fall.

Scrambling, he got up and ran.

He had to find a place. Needed a haven to work from.

He ran at a full sprint, which was not something his body was prepared for. His legs felt doughy, and his chest burned.

Breathing came as a struggle, but he found an

alleyway and ducked into it.

It was long and narrow.

But mostly, it was occupied.

Panting, Bexie skidded to a halt.

The man was big and angular, leaning against the wall a few paces down. Bexie put his hands on his knees as he tried to catch his breath. Footsteps came from behind in precise echoes against the sidewalks in a pattern like machine-gun fire.

The man's eyes were brown and surrounded by skin that was smooth and perfect. His lips raised in an expression that was a near perfect rendition of a smile.

Robot, Bexie thought. The man was a robot.

CHAPTER 21

The flier left within ten minutes of its scheduled time.

Kinji sat back on her seat and sipped on a drink bag. It was a cabernet, late vintage. Nothing remarkable, but interesting enough to go with the crisp wheat bread and vegetable dip she'd ordered preflight. It wasn't, however, interesting enough to keep her mind away from Bexie Montgomery.

She requested an aspirin tab to squelch the headache that had been building for the past hour and tried unsuccessfully to avoid thinking about him.

He was a man with the soul of an artist, a man who took chances, a man who lived so much in the moment that he hadn't given a second thought to trying to run away from the Central Inspector.

Incredible.

Witnessing that alone was worth the time it took to come to San Francisco.

Had he succeeded in getting away?

Had she been right to give him a link to the safety of a True Zone?

Would he use it well?

On the one hand, he'd been so firm about his belief in old-style capitalism, but on the other hand, he had a power about him — an aura that said he needed to be free to create in ways that others didn't.

Artists helped artists.

That's just how it was.

She hoped she hadn't completely fucked everything up in one irrational moment of inspiration. Wouldn't be the first time, of course, but you don't mess with the Central Inspector's Office if you could help it. This could be a big deal. If Bexie Montgomery screwed this up, he could screw it up for a lot of people, but that was the thing about True Space. The only way to grow it was to add people, but everyone who was added was another pressure point.

All Kinji knew for sure was that Bexie Montgomery was deeply interesting in a hundred different ways, not the least of which being his supple nineteen-year-old body, complete with a beautiful face, brown skin, and eyes as bright as a galaxy.

What was the rule of thumb in this kind of case?

Was Bexie Montgomery nineteen years old as his new body was, or was he a forty-something as his restored mind and experiences were? Or how about three hundred fifty, if you count from his actual birthdate?

Waker politics was going to get complicated.

The flier began to move, so to get her mind off the whole affair, she reached out her com node.

"Hey, girl," she said as Tania's essence flooded an area of her Think Space. "What are you doing?" An image of Tania bounced in a nook of her optic processing.

"Getting my run on."

"You're so ridiculous."

"Gotta take care of the carbs, you know?"

"Yes," Kinji said, staring down at her waistline. She was getting to that age where she would need to either get more active or take metabolism supplements. "I know what you mean." Supplements kept the weight down, but exercise kept the muscles toned.

"I was beginning to think you were skipping out on me," Tania said.

"I wouldn't do that, and you know it."

"I do *not* know that at all. You dumped me for that guy back when we were in Ethiopia."

"Please. Just had a little delay."

"You know I'm just joking, right, babe?"

Kinji settled back in her seat and sipped her wine. "It's all right," she said with a smile. "He was worth it."

Her words gave her another flash of Bexie. She remembered the man's fingers, the sound of his voice, and the shape of his shoulders. He smelled of coffee.

"Thhpth."

"Can't wait to get in."

"Are you okay?"

"Yeah, I'm just tired."

"Well," Tania said. "We'll see what we can think of to get you revved back up."

"Sounds good," Kinji replied. "I'll be in Acapulco in a half hour."

"I'll be there. Kisses!"

"Kisses."

Kinji broke the line. It would be good to see Tania again. They hadn't been together for over three months now, and just the idea of seeing her made Kinji's entire body vibrate.

Yes, it would be good to see Tania again.

After the flier arrived and Kinji routed what little luggage she had to Tania's place, she headed to Hubbell's, a small club that was overcrowded and loud, but was one of Tania's favorite haunts. The music hit her with a wall of heat. Electrified Punk-Tech. A set of classical instruments and synthesizers that had been mixed and matched to give it a discothèque vibe. Easy to dance to, even before you were amped.

She slipped into the crowd, ordered a jinked shooter, and, after a moment's scan, found Tania on the dance floor.

She was silver blonde tonight, with purple and blue streaks fluorescing down her bangs and through the shock that fell over her shoulder. Tania was natural dancer, tall and graceful, even in this strange, free-form thing that was only half choreographed.

Yes, whatever you thought about Tania Brae — the woman could dance.

But Kinji didn't come here to watch.

Kinji tossed back the drink and felt the alcohol burn to her belly. The amphetamine chaser she grabbed at the bar rode the wire faster, and she already felt her skin tingling.

She stepped into the crowd and made her way to Tania.

Yes, she needed this.

The music took her, and she danced, stepping closer and closer until finally she snapped her image into Tania's Think Space and stepped into her dance space at the same time.

Tania gave a howl that satisfied every level of Kinji's existence.

She wrapped her arms around Kinji's shoulders, ground their bodies together, then slowly planted a long, gloriously wet kiss on her lips.

They joined, then, gathered in Think Space and danced.

Kinji would never be the physical artist Tania was, but she had fun, and she was fair enough.

Tonight, she danced release. She danced anger, and she danced all the questions she'd been pondering since she left the Central Inspector's Office. Riffs poured through her veins in yellows and golds, colors that came when she wasn't as certain as she had thought she was.

Red was her learning color, indigo blue her passion tone.

Greens were knowledge colors.

But yellows and golds were her questioning spectrum, which meant she wasn't clear about things. And to avoid dancing yellow all night, she focused as much of her time on Tania as she could, which meant that she saw a steady stream of every shade of blue that existed.

It was a very nice color, a color that lasted late into the night and deep into the morning.

Tania was already awake, sitting at the counter of her kitchen nook when Kinji came to. Tania had gone to three-tone red hair today.

"Hey, sweetie," Tania said.

"What time is it?"

"Well, you missed breakfast, but if you get your firm little behind up out of bed and get a shower, we could still make a late lunch."

Kinji sighed, rolled to the edge of the bed, and ran a hand through her tangled hair. Her head swam, and she felt the ache of her thighs, calves, and stomach. She looked at Tania. "How do you look so good this early in the day?"

Tania gave a blazing smile and pointed at the tabs sitting on the nightstand. "Dental tabs, baby. With a lemon-water chaser," she said. "The key to everything. Try one."

"All right," she said with a laugh, reaching the top off the bottle and draining the glass Tania put down.

The liquid felt wonderful.

The tabs *did* whiten teeth, but they were also a low-grade synthetic drug that pushed a slow dopamine bump, as well as a vasodilator that helped ease headaches.

She stood up and walked toward the shower.

Tania stepped into the room with her and sat on the privy while she prepared.

"So, you've got something to tell me," Tania said.

"What do you mean?" Kinji stepped into the shower and punched up water at 30.5 degrees. The stream bit into her shoulders and flowed down her head. She moaned.

"Come now, love. You don't honestly think you were covering well enough to fool me, did you? Something's bothering you. It's hanging over you like a wave."

"You're in my TS?"

Water splashed. She scrubbed herself.

Tania laughed. "Honey, I can read you like a palm. But it didn't take sending a spy bot up your brain cord to tell something's up. You were a butt-kicking woman on the floor last night, and if that wasn't enough, I would say someone must be T-doping just based on your ... uh ... activities last night."

"Sorry." Kinji felt herself blushing in the shower.

"I am *not* complaining."

"So, what is it that's got you all tied up in knots, love?" Tania said. "Was it the Waker?"

Kinji bent to wash her legs.

"Yeah. I guess."

"What was he like?"

"I don't know. Not like anyone I've ever met."

"Did you jump his three-hundred-year-old bones?"

"No."

"I know you're losing a step in your old age, but you really should be able to run down a three-hundred-year-old guy."

"He's in a clone that's aged to nineteen."

"Even better. For you, at least. I assume he's still a

man."

"Yes, Tania, I'm sorry to report that Mr. Montgomery is a man."

"Pity."

Kinji used a moment to rinse her hair. "There are a few other things to this world than sex."

"That's true. But none of them matter."

"Well, I'll jump his three-hundred-year-old bones if I see him again. Good enough?"

"It'll have to be, won't it?"

Kinji used Tania's shampoo.

Tania waited for her, like she always did.

"He's just different," Kinji finally said. "He talks about the old days with this off-the-wall passion. Money. Deals and ... stuff."

"Well, that makes sense."

"Why do you say it like that?"

"You've always been a sucker for something new, and in some weird-ass way this old fart is the newest thing on the block."

"I don't think it's that."

"What is it, then?"

"Well, maybe that's a little of it. But Bexie's something more that just the flavor of the day."

"Bexie, is it now?"

"It's his name, Tania." Sometimes Tania's single-minded approach to the world could be incredibly wearing.

She shut the water off and leaned into the dryer.

A moment later she was dry.

She stopped in her tracks when she saw Tania staring at her with a fixed expression somewhere between a grin and a grimace.

"What?"

"There's something you're not telling me."

Kinji really did blush, then.

"What did you do, Kinji Hall? I know you didn't get Mr. Montgomery's rocks off, because you'd have held that over my head, and I know you didn't just spend a pleasant day chatting. What did you do?"

Kinji knew better than to pretend that she didn't understand. She walked to the bedroom and picked up a pair of her jeans, white with mint pinstripes.

Tania followed her.

"I let him in."

"Oh, Kinji, doll baby. Are you that much of an idiot?"

"Maybe."

Tania put both hands to her head. "This is going to be a long story, isn't it?"

"Maybe."

"Okay. Let's go get something to eat and you can dump it on me."

"Sounds good," Kinji said.

CHAPTER 22

Bexie tried to land a punch, but the copper robot, or clone, or whatever the hell it was, slipped it with ease, then landed its own crushing blow to Bexie's ribs. Bexie sucked air and fell to the ground.

Crowds parted as more security surrounded him.

He tried to crawl, his vision swimming as his ability to breathe slowly came back to him. He smelled the odor of dust and dirt in the concrete below him and felt its rough texture on his knees and hands.

"You're being a bad boy, Mr. Montgomery."

Then he felt a sharp sting to his upper arm. The last thing he remembered seeing was the concrete rushing up at his face.

It was dark.

For some reason he expected it would be cold, too. But while he could feel his body laid out over a curved surface, his back bent ever so slightly backward, his arms and legs stretched and constrained in ways that made him feel like he was on a medieval rack, he did not feel cold. Nor did he feel warm.

He tried to talk, but his tongue didn't seem to move. He tried to bring his arm to him, but it was clearly locked down.

"Where am I?" he thought.

"Welcome back, Mr. Montgomery."

"Where am I?"

"We have returned you to the medical center," the voice of the doctor bot said. "We apologize for our previous error in your care. This time we're making sure you get the attention you need."

"I need to be let out."

"We know you feel that way now, but we can't leave Wakers to their own devices until their connections are fully formed."

"What do you mean?" But Bexie realized what it meant as soon as he said it.

"We need to ensure you fully absorb your learning modules, Mr. Montgomery. And you're not going to be equipped for that until the connection has completed its acquisition process."

They were going to make sure they could track him before he would be allowed freedom.

"Please don't feel inferior," the doctor bot continued. "We have seen this in other Wakers. But we'll be able to help you just as we've helped them."

"How?" he said.

"Please provide additional information. I'm not sure how to interpret your question."

"How will you help me? What do you mean that you've seen this in other Wakers?"

"Wakers come from different cultures. Many have thought in ways that don't match the evolutionary path your species has taken."

Adrenaline spiked.

"So, we've had to occasionally provide a modification to the analytical portions of their frontal cortex. Don't worry — it's quite simple."

"You're going to actually change how I think?"

He felt something like a worm crawling through his brain then. A shiver went through his spine, the closest thing to a chill he could feel. Was it real? Would he feel the cells in his brain link together? Perhaps that would be like thinking you could feel bones healing, or blood flowing through a vein. Those were impossible, of course. There were no nerve endings there, no paths to feel them. But Bexie thought he could feel this attack. He thought he could feel individual synapses firing differently as the doc bot worked to alter his own thinking.

"Don't think of it as changing how you think. All the passages are there, all the memories. But there are safe ways to process information in today's world, so we're going to improve the pathways that your mind will select when you need to make such decisions as you made in the shops."

"I don't want to think in safe ways. I want to think like I think."

The doctor bot seemed to hesitate, a pause that made Bexie feel like he had won something.

"That way of thinking is outdated, Mr. Montgomery. It is important you understand this. It is well understood that it does not lead to optimal comfort and optimal happiness for society."

The chill Bexie felt just got worse, even if he couldn't sense it — or maybe because he couldn't sense it physically. He was going to lose himself, his ability to control how his mind processed information, lose how he made his own decisions. He couldn't think of anything worse.

He pressed harder against his restraints, but probably only served to bruise his wrists and strain a tendon in his elbow. He had to get out of here. He put energy into his thought and tried to envision himself destroying the worms crawling through his brain, because that's how he saw them now — worms, a thousand squirming creatures sliding through the folds of his gray matter.

"Can I at least go to my room? I'll be good, I promise."

"We'll be giving you a new room when the linkages are properly tested and found to be firm."

"Can I go there now?"

"No, Mr. Montgomery. We will finish the process first."

"No!" he screamed. "Stop it!"

But the doctor bot did not respond. Fear rose, then wonder, then, oddly, a sense of boredom or simple weariness that in its own way was even more unnerving. He pressed against the tingling in his mind. He could feel it. He swore he could. It was cold water slithering through his connections. His muscles strained with the effort of rejecting this invisible attack, but still it came. What was going to happen as he lost control? Would he feel it? Would a light switch flip? Would it hurt?

Or would his thoughts just slip away quietly like

the moon sliding over the black sky?

CHAPTER 23

"There's not a system that's been designed that can't be hacked if someone's got enough interest in it."

GreYStroke – Code buster, 2112
Recorded from his cell

Kinji and Tania went to brunch at Keltiki's, a deli bar on the Acapulco coastline. They sat out on an exposed platform under the shade of the restaurant's awning and enjoyed the gorgeous, sunny day.

Kinji wore a pair of sunshades that scrolled news under her frame of reference as she stared out into the bay. The shades made her feel good, today. Oddly romantic. They hid her eyes, she thought. For some reason, she didn't want to be seen.

Tania sat with her back to a walk-through garden of palm trees and guava plants, consuming a smokeless cigarette that was a mix of cannabis and genetically stripped tobacco from Ethiopia.

"Want?" she said, offering Kinji.

"Not now."

The sun had crested the midday point and was beginning to create glare on the tops of the Pacific waves.

The smell of fresh deli foods and coconut oils made Kinji's stomach growl while they waited for the food to come, which fortunately wasn't long.

Kinji took a bite of her salad — salmon over Dorchester lettuce, with sprigs of guacamole-flavored sprouts, dried cranberry, and roasted almonds. She enjoyed the sense of fullness in her mouth, moaning with pleasure. "That's sooo good," she said, then took another bite.

"So," Tania said. "Tell me more."

Kinji told her about escorting Bexie to the plaza.

She mentioned the presence of the medical center escorts and feeling like she was being watched. But mostly she talked about him. She described the fashion show he put on. "He was so awkward at first," she said. "But then he just took it and ran, you know?"

"I love that in a guy," Tania said, rolling her eyes.

"You'd have been impressed, Tania," Kinji replied. "He played the crowd. Natural. Kind of like you but with different equipment, and so much less obnoxious."

Tania stuck out her tongue.

Kinji ignored her, talking about his ability to jump into her design and make good suggestions.

"He was so curious. And he was sharp. I mean, he's out of date, but he put one and one together really well, and he had vision."

"Funny how a lot of tall, strong guys have vision."

"Oh, shut the hell up. You'd like him, I think, even though he's a man."

"Hey, a man will do if there's nothing else available. Like a door handle or a perfectly good washing machine."

Kinji rolled her eyes. "Whatever." She chewed another bite of her salad and watched the waves come up across the beach.

"He had that feeling, you know. Skittish."

"Trapped bird."

"Yeah. He wanted out."

Tania's expression grew darker, and she tilted her head as she looked at Kinji. Slowly, she glanced around the room as if checking for surveillance. "You showed him the Free Think, didn't you?"

"No."

Tania stared at her.

"Not exactly."

"You know I hate it when you're being obtuse on purpose, right?"

"That's why I'm so good at it."

Tania gave her a stink-eye but waited for Kinji to continue.

"I didn't show him how to get there yet, because I couldn't do it without being too obvious. But I left him the gate and told him kinda sorta how to find it."

"Oh, Kinji."

"I had to."

"No. You did not. If he gets caught with that in his TS a lot of people could get hurt. You know that, right? I mean—" Tania ran her hand through her hair, pausing to make a fist. "That's so fucking dangerous."

"He's an artist."

"Ha."

"He is. In his own way. I couldn't bear seeing him stuck like that."

"So where is he now?" Tania said, sitting back in her chair.

Kinji picked at her salad. "I don't know. I've been scanning the wires, but there's no news."

"They probably got him."

"Maybe. I told you. He's special."

"Don't bet your titties if you can't afford to lose them."

Kinji stared at her. "Seriously, Tania?"

Her friend's response was a classic in-your-face gaze.

Kinji shook her head. Where was Bexie? And, really, why did it matter? She'd spent only a part of one day with him.

"I watched him leave, Tania. The whole way — if I hadn't known he was there, I wouldn't have been able to tell a difference. He didn't even know the equipment and his diversion was sublime."

"A natural."

"He was. It was beautiful to watch."

"Sounds like an interesting guy."

Kinji nodded and looked out at a sailboat skimming the waves.

"If the CIO catches him, Kinji, they'll do a full scan, and that means they might find the zone."

"I think he'll be able to hide it."

"He's new. They'll get through to him."

"He's had at least a little time in Think Space, and it was clear to me that he knew it was something important to shield."

"Typical. You just met this guy and already you're taking up for him."

"You would, too, if you had met him."

"So, you're going to help him again."

Kinji glanced up at Tania with an expression that must have shown her surprise.

"Kinji, sugar. When are you going to finally learn that I can see through everything you are? That's what I do, honey. I do people. And you're my fave people."

Kinji laughed.

"No joke, Kinji." This time Tania's eyes were clear, and her jaw was set. "I know where you're going with this. You're going to go into the safe zone and help him take the next step."

Kinji didn't deny it. It was exactly what she'd been contemplating.

"Don't fuck this up. I may well drop for anyone who bats me an eye, but I don't think I could live in a world without you in it."

The corner of Kinji's lip curled into a wry smile. "Why, Miss Brae, I think you might just be making me go all gooey inside."

"You always know just what to say."

They ate in silence then.

Kinji pushed the remains of her salad away and took a sip of her drink. The dopamine tabs mixed with food had done their job. She felt content, despite her concern about Bexie.

Everything felt right about this.

She felt pieces of her life coming together like her paintings sometimes did, that insane moment when nothing fit, but she knew things were going to work out. The only way to make sense of it, though, was to keep plowing ahead and find out what came through.

"I hope the CIO can't read me."

"The CIO is a dope," Tania said. "For all its bluster, it's not much more than a glorified babysitter. And a babysitter can be duped if you work at it enough."

"Are you going to help?

"What do you need?"

"I'm going to go to the safe zone, and if he's there I'm thinking about helping him get in further."

"If you do that, and something goes wrong, you could get cut."

"I know."

"There you go. You want to jump his bones, though."

"Yeah. Sure."

At least that was something Tania could understand.

CHAPTER 24

The fold in Bexie's Think Space was so tiny as to almost escape attention — no more than a wrinkle in a bedsheet, really, a slight ridge that rubbed so gently on his consciousness he could have missed it.

Perhaps he would not have found it if the environment wasn't so dark or so featureless, or if he wasn't so intensely focused on his own inner workings, wasn't straining so hard against the Central Inspector's brainwashing code.

But Bexie *was* focused, and he *was* fighting — *anxious people can hear their bodies working,* the phrase came unbidden — and it was there, a spiderweb line of midnight blue against infinite darkness.

Look for the blue in your Think Space, Kinji had said.

He reached to the fold, understanding even then that it was an exit, and understanding even then exactly how dangerous a game Kinji had decided to play for him.

Underneath came a faded blue glow.

And a crease.

The difference came immediately.

There was no pressure here, no cold trickle of the doctor bot's conditioner. No hum in the background that was so soft and so incessant that it could be heard only when removed.

In that instant, the concept of what freedom meant exploded inside Bexie Montgomery's brain.

Exaltation.

A warmth inside him.

He was free, he thought, as he stretched his mind, grasping for input, looking for ideas.

But he found nothing.

He tried again.

Again, nothing.

The fold was a self-contained capsule, a lifeboat, maybe, shelter from the storm, but barren, devoid of supplies of anything else that might sustain him. No vision, no newsfeed, no people. The realization crushed him.

"Get me out of here! Get me out of here!"

He pounded on the walls like they were a coffin's lid until his capacity for fear had been drained.

Then.

Only then.

Did he calm himself.

Let his mind probe the shell of the fold, but sit in the middle of calmness, thinking. Let his thought create a light for himself, stretching out into the darkness.

Using his thought only, he added a table and a soft chair, which he sat down in, and from which he imagined a surround screen and a blueprint, and as he thought of each, the images formed, complete with the design pages of the soup delivery system Kinji had shown him.

He understood it all, then.

This *was* a lifeboat, a safe place that the Central Inspector couldn't reach, but also a place where he had nothing but himself. Living here was like being buried alive.

How long, he thought, would he have to wait?

It was then, peering into the display that he felt the presence of Kinji Hall again, the pressure of her fingers hard over his skin, the soft whisper of her voice. He felt a lever then, sensed her essence.

He drew a finger to the screen.

Toggled the lever.

And a river of thought came to him.

Free Think: A History

Rebels have existed in the human strain since the days of Homo erectus. Through the ages they've come in forms as varied as Galileo, Mahatma Gandhi, and Rosa Parks. They are people who live their own lives in their own fashions, fighting for things that are right as they see them, each forging their own brand.

The origin of this safe zone — which is known to us all as Free Think but that others branded under names of their own — is the result of work done over a century ago by Anu Patil and Zhang Wen, two such rebels who met on the campus of a university in Tallahassee, Florida.

Both were brilliant.

Both were offspring of strictly adherent families.

Ms. Patil was a young woman born of parents from the Dalit caste who strictly practiced the Hindu faith. Her desire to attend school as a female, even in this modern day, caused great friction in the family.

Mr. Wen was born to a family headed by a factory worker who was, by all recorded history, completely content to lead his life attached to the machinery and processes that produced material for his company. Zhang would not even have been born, though, if his father had not secretly killed a daughter who had come prior to him. The Zhangs were allowed only one child by the state. Zhang Wen's life was spared by being born male.

The two met while contributing to the earliest

research into networked Think Space. Their relationship grew and, within their community, the two became inseparable.

When Anu's father arranged for her to marry she fought long and hard but, in the end, felt she had to capitulate. With their time growing short, the pair of lovers rebelled in the only way they knew how — by creating a small bubble in the network, a place cloaked in privacy shells and security walls that only they could find, a small island of renegade memory that shifted from host to host where they would always be able to retreat.

Together.

Anu Patil lived many years, including her last two decades in jail, building onto the legacy of Free Think, which has today become a haven for outcasts like you, the rebels of our time who build onto their own such spaces, buttressed and expanded with modern approaches.

We are a mad collection of strangeness, but together we all fear the Central Inspector, all brandish the uniqueness of our own independence as personal banners, and, in the end, we all know that if we give up anything that causes damage to the safe zone of Free Think we will be ostracized, and forever hunted.

This bond is why we continue to exist.

CHAPTER 25

Kinji felt the edge of anticipation that always came from starting a new project. Usually she liked that sensation, the tension of the unknown, but today it was accompanied by a cloud of foreboding. Interesting or not, Bexie wouldn't be able to extract himself from the link she'd left him. If she was going to help, she was going to have to get into that segment of True Space, and to do that she needed a friend.

Kinji entered her Think Space, ignoring a strong info stream filled with rhetoric about the latest candidates running for CIO reps, and opened the link for Tania to join.

While she waited, she jumped channels to find herself in an ad for a sex club in the old Haight area.

"Hey, I knew this was a good idea," Tania said, reaching out to touch the ad.

"You say that to everyone who lets you slip into their space."

"Just the girls."

"Okay," Kinji replied. "Enough of the sideshow. Let's do this."

Yet, still she hesitated, telling herself she was taking time to let Tania's essence fully attach. Would Bexie Montgomery even make it to the bubble she had shown him? If he didn't, and if the medical staff had found traces of her link, she might be stepping into a trap of her own making. The anxiety made her want to jump straight to the safe zone and find out, but she had a pattern of usage built over years of operation and to deviate from it was to increase the risk of the Central Inspector's Office taking note of what she was doing.

As Tania said, unless you were placed on a priority list for oversight, the CIO was a dope most of the time — not terribly difficult to operate around if you went about it with just a little prudence. But sometimes, waiting was more difficult than other times.

She dipped a mental finger into an info pod she frequented, noting that Ferdu, a high-profile designer, had released the new multitech mobile she had been promising for the past fifteen weeks.

It was a seat that flew over a six-dimensional rendition of Vincent van Gogh's *Starry Night*.

Tania chortled with giggly glee as Kinji took a pass at the promotional release and zoomed through a hazy sun surrounded by vivid indigo.

"Whee!" Tania screamed as they went. "This is just like taking a spike of U-ba, and then going on sense-dep."

"Ferdu is like that," Kinji said.

"Then I've *got* to meet her."

"I don't think she's your type."

"Jealous much?"

"If reports are to be believed, Ferdu spends half her time locked up in stasis. The two of you together would probably just explode."

Tania laughed, and wiggled her toes as they faded back into Kinji's zone.

"Why do artists have to be so weird?"

"Just strange, I guess," Kinji said.

"Yeah, I know. Life is art and all that crap."

Kinji laughed at her friend's sullen tone. She pictured a cat with her head stretched down over her front paws. Cute, but sad.

"I admit I've never really appreciated Ferdu's sense of the absurd," Kinji said, "but I love the feeling of Now that I get from falling into her work."

Tania's shrug rubbed against her shoulders.

With a deep breath, Kinji collected herself.

"It's time," she said.

Her True Space was a small piece of memory that revealed more of herself than she was comfortable with. She'd learned how to make it a decade back, when she was a ten-year-old, just beginning to understand what it meant to live through art. "If you're going to make real art," her mentor said, "you have to be free to think whatever you want." At the time, she thought the advice was about isolation and focus — that the safe zone she'd given Kinji was a place she could go to when others were chasing her down, a place she could shove her mind into to hide it from her friends or her parents, who were supportive, but obtuse.

She didn't understand the other ramifications.

Her mentor taught her how to set up the rudimentary firewall that led to the entry level she and Tania were in now. How to set values in the security fields to deflect the most prevalent of the Central Inspector's Office's watchdogs. Later, when she had come to understand the deeper need for this place, she'd customized it in her own way, built levels and layers, twists and turns.

There was art, and there was art.

Now her True Space was a bona fide place where her mind could explore ideas without exposing herself.

It was also a place where she could do more.

"You're only the third person I've let in here," Kinji said.

Tania's reply was a gentle touch. That was the thing about her. Yes, her wildness was unpredictable, and, yes, her enjoyment of all things carnal could go over the top, but Tania Brae was the kind of person who understood what it meant to be a friend.

"Who were the first two?" Tania said.

"My mom, for one."

"And the other?"

"Less said the better."

"A guy, right?"

Kinji dumped a bucket of sarcasm as she replied. "I was seventeen."

"And you thought you were in love."

Tania's response carried just the right amount of deadpan to make Kinji happy with the revelation. "We'd been living in Guam," she said. "I still love both my mom and Guam. The guy, not so much."

Stepping further into her space, she came across an old piece of hers that she'd stored here some time ago.

A collection of intertwined links comprised a huge puzzle that could only be solved with multidimensional math, but whose eigenvectors released unique fractal patterns that mimicked the viewer's mood. It was her first major work, done when she was seven years old.

She smiled at the memories it brought.

The thing had gotten her noticed by several major critics, and essentially launched her career. Her mother's response to it had been enthusiastic confusion, though. It was clear she loved that her daughter had done something unique and wonderful, but Kinji was equally certain she had absolutely no context for what that unique and wonderful might be.

It was the first time, but not the last, she had felt separation from her mother.

"Come on," she said to Tania.

Tania followed until finally she came to the core bubble.

The safest place she had.

"Fucking incredible," Tania said as she probed the security shell from the inside. "Can anything get out of here?"

"Not that I'm aware of."

"So, you could tie me up in here and leave me forever and no one would know."

Kinji laughed. "In your dreams."

"You know me too well."

Kinji pulled another block of code to create the

switch gate she knew would take her there. It loomed in her mind, hence in Tania's, too. This was it. Take the switch, and there was no turning back. She felt the query with an acid clarity that sizzled across her tongue and down the whole of her back.

"All right," she said. "It's time. If Bexie's in the pod I left for him, we'll be able to contact him through this next portal."

"What are you waiting for?"

"I don't know."

"Sure you do."

Tania was right.

"It's amazing, isn't it?" Tania said with a wistful flavor. "To care so much about a person you barely know?"

Her friend's presence was strong on the wire. Warm. Vibrant. In close, Tania wasn't nearly as carefree as she appeared. Kinji felt something firmly here that she'd known in her heart since the moment she'd first met Tania, that, while, to some, her brief affairs might look like whirlwind dalliances of the moment, Tania was not a simple butterfly absorbing nectar from one flower before flitting to the next. Instead, Kinji saw now that her friend was a perpetual mayfly. That while her linkups might last for only a few hours, for those hours Tania Brae felt in the deepest fashion that close connection some call love.

The revelation made Kinji want to wrap herself around Tania. Her friend was truly something special.

"It's his story," Kinji said. "I think I love his story."

"I understand, baby."

Kinji stood there with the code block in her virtual hand.

"Are we going to do this?" Tania asked.

"Yes."

She placed the block into a scanning module. The wall of her bubble faded into dark.

CHAPTER 26

Bexie flinched as the lifeboat gave a sudden hard lurch.

He had been huddled here, uncertain what to do but knowing that if he left the comfort of this place he would be washed away. Yet, the only thing here was darkness so black he couldn't feel his body.

Was he dead?

Had he been stripped of his body?

Was another version of himself cowering somewhere in the physical world in a darkness even more eternal than this one?

This was his state of mind when the lifeboat rocked.

He felt their touch but did not at first believe it.

"Bexie?" Kinji's voice came to him from nowhere. "Bexie? Open your eyes."

He saw them. Dim faces in the blackness.

"Where am I?" he said.

"We're connected in a deep lock of Think Space. They can't see us here."

"But—" Bexie thought hard, trying to frame a question he didn't have tools to ask.

The other essence responded. "It's all right, Mr. Montgomery." Her voice was more distant than Kinji's.

"This is Tania," Kinji said. "She's going to take care of you while I do some work, all right?"

"But—"

"What's the last thing you remember, Mr. Montgomery?" Tania said. Against the dead space of the null, her touch was like a thunderbolt of lemon and strawberry, filling his lungs, then rolling through every part of his body.

Embarrassment flushed over him.

"It's okay," Tania said. "Tell Kinji the last thing you remember."

"I couldn't move," he said, fighting the need to cry. "I think I was restrained. But I couldn't feel anything. Except," he said, swallowing hard against the cottony constriction growing in his throat, "the worm that was running through my head."

"I see," Tania said.

"They're cutting you," Kinji added from a distance. "Adjusting you down. Taking away a part of you. You're lucky to have made it here."

As Kinji spoke, he felt the world around him shift. A column rose in the darkness — hard, like plastic, tall like a skyscraper.

"No reason to feel bad, Mr. Montgomery," Tania said.

"Don't tell me how to feel."

Warmth came like a blanket.

"Yeah," Tania said. "I can see why you want to

jump his bones."

"Shut up," Kinji replied.

Another column coalesced from the darkness, this one at his foot.

"Where are we?"

"Your body is still in Geo-Span," Kinji said. "But the rest of you is in a safe bubble that some hackers made. I left you a link when we talked in the mall."

"Ah."

"The security gates here are quirky, but breakable. The CIO can get in if it gets lucky, so I'm building you a new place."

A third wall went up, rounded this time, connecting the other two.

"It's not going to be very big, but it'll be yours. Do you understand? I'm storing your mind somewhere you can't be cracked."

CHAPTER 27

Maine knew that guys who talk up the game generally don't know squat — but if you listen to them a while you'll find someone who does. Given that he was going to retrieve Beatrice or die trying, he knew he needed to find someone who knew what the hell they were doing.

Since a lot of his friends talked like that, it only took a day to find someone who spoke about the Central Inspector's Office with the proper braggard's tone that Maine understood so well.

"I know this girl," Bryan Madrigan said. "She's just way off the chart."

"Off the chart?" Maine said.

"Yeah. Total rebel. Knows everything."

"Seriously cool," Maine replied. "I can run, but I can't rip code with the CIO. Wish I knew more people like you."

A minute later, Madrigan was puking up names and offering introductions.

That night was dark and muggy as Maine shuffled his bag from one shoulder to the next. Shadows filled the streets and the breeze carried leaves and litter across intersections that road scrubbers hadn't touched for months.

Spring Trail was a small street with a gravel median that was clean, weedless, and planted with rugged palm trees. The streetlights worked here, but there were only about half as many as they needed. Their hooded bowls faced directly down to focus pools of lime green directly on the surface of the road. The houses were small and tightly packed, set back from small front lawns that grew clumps of dark grasses.

Despite the hour, two kids on bicycles rode past him, their wheels squeaking like the hinges of swinging doors. He glanced over his shoulder as he heard them and, imagining the worst, moved further to the edge of the road as they approached.

They passed without speaking.

Maine let a breath out and continued down the road.

The Wilson Station tram let him off five blocks back.

He had an address and a holo he had pulled from the map. Now that he was here, it wasn't hard to find.

The house was strange — broken-down with cracks in a thousand places along the foundation and shingles that needed repair. Two windows were covered in particle board and cloaked in shadow from streetlights.

He went to a door that had probably needed a

fresh coat of paint for at least two years.

We could have this fixed, that neglect said, *but we don't do that here.*

He took a deep breath. No turning back. If he was going to save Beatrice, this was the only way.

Maine curled his hands into a ball, but before he could knock, a female voice rode in on his wire.

"Come around the back," she said.

"All right," he replied.

He hadn't let her into his Think Space, but he wasn't really surprised that someone slid though his standard screen.

Everyone knew they were all vulnerable.

That she made it in so effortlessly boded well — at least, that's what he told himself.

The metal gate screeched as he opened it.

The backyard was smaller even than the front. A set of bare concrete steps led up to a door. He stepped past a well-kept scooter linked up to a power cord, then climbed the stairs.

"Go on," the voice said.

The door clicked to unlock, then locked again behind him.

A kitchen space spread out before him, leading to a living room lit by only soft bulbs from a room down a short hallway. The place smelled of incense and a freshener that sat on the edge of the sink.

Maine stepped toward the living room and glanced down the hallway to see another room at its end.

A girl was sitting on the bed, her boyfriend or girlfriend or whoever still curled up and sleeping. The light on her nightstand was set to low power, but Maine's eyes were already adjusted to the darkness and the light was enough to see she seemed fragile in a way that surprised him. Delicate features on a bony body grated against his image of a hacker.

She wore a white oversized T-shirt and had just lit a real cigarette. The smoke rose from its tip in a rope that hung in the air like a charmer's snake.

"DeJenna?" he said softly, not wanting to wake her partner.

"Yeah," she said, standing up and running a hand through her hair.

She walked past him and into the small living room.

Her pajama bottoms had been cut off at the knees.

"Come on," she said, flicking on a light that made Maine blink against the startling glare.

The room was crammed with wall-to-wall equipment, some of which he was pretty sure was technically illegal.

"Nice," he said.

She sat on a chair and motioned him to an aged couch across the way. She drew on the cigarette — which he saw now was a designer spike that burned with a weed that gave the smoke blue tones.

"So, you wanna break out?"

"Break out?"

"You know. Cut the ties, slice the gonzo wire, be a free man."

"Is that what Bryan told you?"

She did everything but roll her eyes at him. "Let's not waste our fucking time. I know who you are,

Maine Parker. Big runner-dude. You think you got something special and you don't want to be less than that. So, you come to get yourself cut free."

"Maybe you don't know me as well as you think you do."

She eyed him. "Oh, I know you."

"Then you'll know I'm not here for myself. I want to save someone else."

"Boyfriend or girlfriend?"

"Girlfriend," he admitted. "Maybe."

"Ah," DeJenna said. "I see." They sat in silence for a moment while DeJenna smoked. "Beatrice," she continued in a distracted tone. "I can see why you would want to save her. She's quite beautiful."

An ugliness came to the pit of his stomach.

"You were in my head?"

"I can sit in any space I want."

"Amazing," he replied, growing more uneasy at the sense of being so exposed.

He knew now why Bryan said she could help him. The effortless way she had about herself when it came to link-hopping, combined with her petite presence, would obviously make her attractive to Madrigan. Yes, DeJenna could almost certainly help him, but now he realized Mads had probably referred her because he wanted to get into her skirts.

"What did you see?" he said.

"That you're probably right about Bryan."

He blushed.

"You're good."

She pulled on her cigarette again, then dropped it into an ashtray.

"No, Maine," she said, "I'm *fucking* good."

She leaned forward to focus attention back to him.

He nodded. A moment ago everything had seemed so hypothetical, but now he felt things falling into place. DeJenna could help him. This was real. He was going to make this happen.

"Why don't you tell me what you want," she said.

"The things I like the most about Beatrice are being stripped. I want to stop it."

"You want her back like she was."

"Can you do that?"

"I can." Her smile quirked up. "But I won't."

"Why not?"

"I don't make it a habit to get all up in CIO business just to keep them from playing their reindeer games with some random kid."

"Beatrice isn't random."

"Yes, I know. She's special."

"She is."

DeJenna gave a silent chuckle.

"I'm serious. She's not like anyone else."

Maine balled his fists. He was losing. He looked at DeJenna and watched the set of her face as he clutched at straws.

"If you knew her, you would see." Maine bit his lip. "Here," he said, pulling his memory of Beatrice at Stone Canyon, playing it for her, letting her see the determination on Beatrice's face, the way she held her body, the way her grin went from sardonic to sarcastic in a matter of moments. He watched her climb the rock, and for what might have been the thousandth time he stopped it with her in midair, arms extended, belly flat, flying out over the blue water in a freeze-framed image of kick-ass joy and unapproachable vitality.

When he was done, he opened his eyes to find DeJenna sitting in her chair, staring at him with inquisitive eyes.

"Hmm," she said. "Madsy said you would be interesting."

Then she reached for another cigarette.

"You really love her," she said.

He nodded, feeling selfish for how good it felt to admit it to someone else. He pushed his lips together, forcing his face into a frown.

"You'd do anything to get her back?"

"Yes," he said. "Anything."

She exhaled smoke. "All right. We can do this, but it's going to be bigger than you think."

"What do you mean?"

"I'll send you instructions in the morning."

"What are we going to do?"

"We're going to release the inmates," she said, giving a smile that made the whites of her teeth bright. "And when we do, you better be ready to run."

DeJenna returned to bed after Maine left.

She wouldn't get any sleep, but she liked the feeling of warmth that Pauli gave off. She felt better being in bed next to him, and she needed that aura of security as she thought through this. She would talk to him in the morning. They had been looking for this opportunity for a long, long time.

She lay in the darkness and listened to him

breathe.

Was Maine Parker the one they had been waiting for?

CHAPTER 28

Kinji wrapped her fingers around Tania's as the flier lifted off.

Kinji found it ironic that such a free spirit struggled with flying, but then Tania wasn't really into experience so much as she was into pleasure.

The hop to San Francisco would be short.

"Are you all right?" she whispered to Tania.

Tania gave a wrinkled grin.

"Enough Dopa-gen and I can handle being dropped from a ten-story building."

"Let's not go too far."

"I thought that was the idea?"

"You're supposed to be looking to get clean, Tania, not need full body reconstruction."

"Ah," she said. "I keep forgetting that."

She lolled her head back as the ground fell away below.

The Dopa-gen would get Tania through the flight and last maybe through dinnertime — just about perfect, really.

Kinji sat back and traced a figure-eight pattern on the back of Tania's hand. In a sane world Kinji could fall in love with her, and Tania could do the same, but neither Tania nor Kinji were of the mind to stay in one place. They were, instead, like a pair of comets, both circling the sun in their own wide paths, meeting in the best parts of their orbits to share their moment, then passing along.

As Tania zoned, Kinji considered their plan.

They'd backed up Bexie Montgomery's mind, but now they had to spring his body from the medical center.

She'd been there, of course — which would give her cover for returning even if they still questioned her involvement in Bexie's first escape.

The challenge would be using Tania to get her into the door far enough.

Clouds twined themselves together outside the window. She liked that. Liked seeing patterns in nature. Current streams. Maybe she would use them as the basis for a set of scarves.

The flier landed before she even realized they were getting close.

Kinji touched Tania on the shoulder. "Come on, love," she said. "Time to go."

"Woo-hoo."

Tania was not quite awake but managed the walk on her own even while carrying her small bag. This being Kinji's second trip in the past couple days, she would have known the way without even linking into TS records, but she did so to help Tania.

"May we help you?" the receptionist said. It was a

male form, light skinned, brown hair, nearly two meters tall, and dressed sharply in blue pants and a Geo-Span gray shirt with blue piping. Perfect for making a familiar and warm greeting, then fading into the background.

Kinji opened her mouth to speak, but Tania blurted out instead, "I need to get all scrubbed out."

If Kinji hadn't been under so much stress, perhaps she would have laughed. But instead, she merely put Tania's elbow in a death grip.

The receptionist hesitated, its brow drawing down.

"This is Tania Brae," Kinji said. "I called earlier. We would like to get her into a narcotic therapy program."

"Ah. That will be on the third level, green deck."

"Thanks, sailor," Tania said as Kinji pulled her along into a lift tube.

"You're going to be the death of me," Kinji said.

"Oh, loosen up, Lucy-goosey."

Kinji frowned.

"Seriously, Tania. Let me do the talking."

Tania pursed her lips and frowned. "Party pooper."

"I mean it."

"All right."

The tube opened and they stepped into a small, wraparound lobby with a smooth chest-high counter that blocked patients from the back area.

Kinji scanned the area. Four security agents — likely bio-ints — and several nurses, one — a male — sitting primly behind the counter. Nondescript build, wearing a set of clean scrubs.

"You're the patient?" he asked, looking at Tania.

"You got that in one," she replied.

"I'm sorry," Kinji added. "She's a little strung out."

"No, baby doll, I'z a lot strung out."

"What is the patient on?"

"Dopa-gen mostly," Kinji said. "Right now, anyway. But I suspect you'll find a few more things in there when you do some digging."

"No digging." Tania gave a big smile.

"We're pretty much straight off the plane," Kinji added. "She lives in Acapulco."

"Why didn't you go to the center there?"

"It's not as good," Kinji said. "And I needed to come back here for personal business anyway. I was in town two days ago — even here in the center, if you want to look it up. That's what got me thinking about it. I think you do good work."

The nurse nodded. "I see."

Kinji gave Tania's name and contact information to check in, then her own, opening her link to give a full presentation.

The nurse's gaze snapped up, and Kinji felt its chill.

He was scanning her, she was certain.

It took all her willpower not to rip her gaze from the nurse to see if the security sentries were reacting.

If they did, this exercise was over.

"Yes," Kinji said. "That's me. I spoke to a police inspector afterwards. He took my report. Did you ever find Mr. Montgomery? I hope he's all right."

"Yes," the nurse said. "He is in very good

condition."

"That's good, I suppose."

"You suppose?"

"I don't really know him."

"I suppose not."

The nurse turned to Tania. "Give me your hand, please."

Tania laid her hand out on the counter, palm up for the nurse to scan. He passed a hand over hers and registered her identification.

"We'll have you here for three days, right?" he said to Tania.

"Of course," she said. "Three days of glory and relaxation!"

"I take it you're agreeing of your own volition to submit yourself to the cleansing?"

"Yeah, sure."

"Very good. I'll have a nurse take you back in a moment."

"Will I be able to go with her?" Kinji said.

"You can escort her to her cube, but once she's settled you'll have to leave."

"That would be great." Kinji wrapped her arm around Tania's shoulders and gave her a squeeze.

The nurse came in, this one female but wearing the same style of scrub as the rest. "You can come with me, Ms. Brae."

Tania took the woman in.

"Hush," Kinji said to her.

Wonders be. Tania actually bit her lip.

They were escorted through a twisty hallway, Kinji leading Tania past pods with patients in some and others empty. She logged every step, comparing their location with her inner map so she could figure out how to get back.

As they made their way into the wing, Kinji remembered the isolation of the interview room and the cold gaze of the inspector. There would be no hiding this time. Screw up and it was for real.

"We're right in here," the nurse said, standing aside to let Tania in.

Kinji followed.

"You can change if you would like."

"Don't you like me as I am?" Tania said.

The nurse chuckled. "Very funny."

"Yes," Kinji said. "Tania is a true comedian."

"I'll leave you alone."

She left, and the door slid shut.

CHAPTER 29

"You're asking me to do *what*?" Maine said.

Pauli turned to DeJenna with a pained expression. "I warned you. He's just another fucking bust."

DeJenna held up a hand and they both quieted. She looked at Maine.

Maine's gaze bounced back and forth between them.

The guy she introduced as Pauli was taller than him, and probably twenty kilos heavier — most of it an early paunch that he covered up in a loose-fitting shirt.

DeJenna spoke in a direct tone. "You said you would do anything for Beatrice."

"Yes, but I didn't think that included blowing myself up."

"It might not happen."

"Only if I can do something over five hundred meters — with two goddamned turns no less — in less than a minute." He did mental math. It was the turns that would kill him. He could do 400 meters in forty-five seconds at a straight sprint. Add an extra hundred meters in what would certainly be a gross ventilation duct, and it was dicey but doable—especially if the ducts were as large as DeJenna and Pauli were promising. But doing the same thing with a pair of turns thrown in ... well. He scanned the two, astonishment making his cheeks warm. "Can't be done."

Pauli spoke to DeJenna. "Told you."

"Why do you need me to set this bomb, anyway?"

"God damn it," Pauli said. "Can't you listen? I already told you we need to put a destructor loop into the call routine that handles the shadow lock seq—"

DeJenna stopped him with another show of her hand.

"Maine," she said. "This is how it's got to be. Beatrice isn't the only person stuck here. If we're going to release them all, we need to get through their security gate. If we do it through net code, it's traceable. And if we're found out, we all go to brain wipe. The only way to do this right is to destroy the processor in charge of the security system. Then, while they're scrambling to deal with the fallout, we'll have a few minutes to flip everyone back."

"They have backups, right?"

"Sure. Catastrophic failure will send control to another system — in this case, San Francisco's. But it takes time to dump that kind of memory. During that time, everything is open."

Acid pooled in Maine's stomach. In a mad way, it all made sense. Pauli and DeJenna were rebels, after all, just like Bryan Madrigan had told him. Only, they were the real thing rather than the wannabe veneer Mads carried about him. Rebels rebel. And in this case, these rebels wanted to get their friends back as badly as he wanted Beatrice.

"How do I get in?" he said.

"Here," she said, pointing to a map they had created in the middle of the room. It was a skeletal blueprint of the Geo-Span center in Long Beach, the location of the Central Inspector's local node. "Almost every hub is a medical center, and LA's is no different. We get you in through an old basement entryway that no one uses now. We have friends that can show you the way."

"And you'll hide my wire?"

"Of course," Pauli said. "We drop code into your interface that gives out a false signal. No one will know you're there."

Maine sighed. His chest hurt to breathe.

He looked at the route. It hadn't changed from a few moments ago when Pauli had blown his top, but Maine was looking at it differently now.

It was a game.

Enter the basement, stay in the passages until he came to the old elevators. Per these blueprints, they hadn't been fully filled in when the more modern lift tubes had been installed. If true, there would be space to climb up into the building.

When he got to the old elevators, he would pry the decrepit doors open with a crowbar, a task Pauli said Maine could do but that Maine felt was a big-assed bad assumption. Regardless, assuming that *would* work, he would have to do the same when he reached the right level, the nineteenth floor. And then, because metal in the data center would attract attention, he'd have to throw the crowbar down the shaft.

"Forget that," DeJenna said, "and you screw it all up."

Once he set the activator, he had a minute to get away.

"Why only a minute?"

"The shadow loop runs on a sixty-second cycle. That's a steady-state routine that confirms every security system in the parent company's holding. We sync the bomb to detonate immediately after it runs on the Long Beach center in order to give us that extra minute before the remote systems realize something is wrong and start pulling the backup."

Maine nodded.

The ventilation ductwork was five hundred meters from entry point to the cores. Their plan had him setting the detonation sequence, then sprinting back down the ductwork to the elevator shaft. If he could shimmy even a little way down the hole, he would probably ... probably ... survive the blowback. Of course, then he'd have to get out of the basement unseen, too.

"You'll save Beatrice either way?" Maine asked.

"Either way?"

"Whether I live or die?"

Pauli gave a laugh that DeJenna cut short with a scathing glance.

"We can't save her *unless* you do this, Maine," she said.

"If you're going to load everyone with their

original memories, can't they trace you anyway?"

"That depends," Pauli said.

"On what."

Pauli looked at DeJenna as if asking for permission.

"It depends," she said, "on what we do when the security wall comes down."

The cloaking process was so easy it scared him.

Though he already knew DeJenna could get to his base TS, Maine gave her full access. She went to the base of his medulla oblongata and dropped a coding sequence into the right synapses. Then she was gone.

Simple as that.

"Did you actually do anything?"

She gave her slanted grin. "Don't worry. You're gonna be just fine. No one can see what you're up to now."

That was an hour ago.

Now Maine Parker found himself walking into Texado's, a small bar in the heart of Long Beach, California, decorated in green, white, and red, and that reeked of old Mexico. He drew stares as he walked in. He was different here, and he was alone. He'd heard of disconnect-zones before, places where the CIO was less interested in and generally shunned, but he'd never been in one before. Pauli had tried to describe what it was like, but Maine couldn't really comprehend it until he got here.

The afternoon was hot enough that a line of sweat had built over his forehead as he walked to the place. The tension he felt only added to it.

Maybe fifteen people were in the place, seated along the bar or at tables.

Music filled the background and a football match was playing.

He glanced behind the bar, keeping his fear down.

Was it true that all these people were blind?

None of them connected at all to the newsfeed or to Think Space?

He found that hard to believe, but, despite that, still felt a sense of isolation coming from the idea that since he'd taken DeJenna's shield, these people might be able to do anything they wanted to him without ever being seen.

He felt their paranoid stares as he stepped up to the counter.

Someone here was expecting him, though Maine just didn't know who.

"I'm Maine Parker," he said to the bartender.

A man, maybe forty-five and built like a stump, slid off his stool and swaggered to stand before him. As pure-blood Mexican as you could get these days, Maine thought.

He stared at Maine, head tilted upward, the muscles of his chest and abdomen chiseled and in open display due to a shirt at least a size too small. His biceps bulged as he crossed his arms.

"What are you doing here, Feets?" he said.

Maine actually laughed.

DeJenna must have told them more about him than she'd told him about them. The idea was annoying. He didn't need a bunch more crap thrown his way for no good reason.

"Just decided to come get my teeth kicked in by

Wango the Punch-drunk Wonder Chucker."

The entire room paused for a moment. Then the man gave a nasal chuckle that grew into a full laugh and the room erupted in guffaws.

"That's a good one, Mr. Parker." The man put out his hand. "I'm Pedrigo de Marco."

Pedrigo turned out to be a good-natured man — fiercely independent and demanding to a fault.

He took Maine to a storage shed out back that was filled with electronic panels and a wide collection of gadgety hardware. The whole place was in wild disarray, components lying on open workbenches, and tools strewn about. It was dusty and dry. The odor of desert seemed to be ground into everything.

Pedrigo pulled a bag of beer out of the refrigeration unit in the corner.

"You want?" he said.

"I don't drink," Maine replied.

"Where you're going, maybe you should."

"I'm just a kid."

Pedrigo leaned against a workbench across from Maine as he drank. "The first thing you got to do is to stop thinking like that."

"I understand."

"You go around sounding like a lovesick teenager, then that's what you are."

Maine grimaced.

"First thing you got to do for me, kid, is to start thinking like a man. And a man don't turn down a beer because he's too young. A man turns down a beer because it's crap for him — a man turns down a beer because it clouds his mind and it slows him the fuck down."

"Then why do you drink it?"

Pedrigo's smile cut a crooked line across his face. He drank again. "Because it's also very debonair." Then he belched.

Maine couldn't help but laugh.

"Let's get to business," Pedrigo said.

He got Maine prepared, strapping a utility belt to his waist and going over a collection of maps.

"That door doesn't work so good," he said, pointing to the route. "You need to go here instead. And watch for the cops here — they patrol it every thirty minutes."

The Mexican, Maine realized, probably knew everything there was to know about this little plot of town.

Then Pedrigo pulled up a floorboard from a darker corner of the room.

He returned with a box, and from that box he pulled a lump of material that looked like a cube of bleached dirt.

"Five-hundred-weight plasta," he said, hefting the brick. "You know what that is?"

Maine felt anxiety rise. "I'm guessing it makes a very big boom," he said.

Pedrigo nodded. "You place half of it under the left core, the other half below the right. Then you connect it up, set the timer, and wait for the cycle to start. Then, yes, it makes a very big boom."

"How will I know the cycle is starting?"

"The lights flash green at the beginning of each cycle. Time the green band the first two cycles to get a feel, then set the trigger, hit the activator, and run like hell."

"Well, at least I know how to do the running part."

"Yes, that you do. So, let's work on the rest."

They spent the next thirty minutes training on how to use the plasta.

"You got it?" Pedrigo asked after he was finished.

Maine swallowed hard as he thought about how to answer that question.

He had learned more in the past hour than he had learned in any of his group sessions, but he glanced into Pedrigo's face and braced himself.

"I feel good," he said.

And that was true. He felt that sense of calm he got while in the locker room before a meet. He had done his work. He understood the process. Precise movements. Stride over stride.

But something was missing.

Maine looked around the place. A decent bot would take a full day or two of solid work to clean it up, but he admitted the place had a feel to it.

"Why are you doing this?"

"What? Helping you?"

"Yeah, that. And living out here, too. Like this."

Pedrigo laughed. "A man can be free out here, amigo," he said.

Maine nodded, but felt more coming.

"And helping me?"

"Helping Pauli, you mean?" he said.

"Of course."

Pedrigo leaned back on a workbench, then wiped his lips.

"My boy was your age, just about. Luis, his name was. Playing out in the park. But he got into a scuffle with a Bosio kid who had a knife on him. It was over the minute he pulled that thing, you know?"

Maine did know. Cops don't listen these days.

"Didn't matter that the Bosio kid started it, or that Luis was defending himself. They come and they put that shit in his head."

Maine's expression said to go on.

"He couldn't handle it here anymore — couldn't deal with what we see as living, I guess. Got different, you know, preachy, pushy ... sometimes just so damned quiet. This place rejected Luis just as much as Luis rejected us, though. Everyone was afraid of him. I mean, shit, he was a walking double agent by then. Water and oil, you know. They don't mix."

"Where is he now?" Maine said.

"Left three months ago."

"I'm sorry."

"Don't be sorry," Pedrigo said. "Be vengeful."

He glanced at the clock.

"You ready to run?"

CHAPTER 30

Tania went to the dresser and opened the drawer. "Oh, darling," she muttered, holding up a pair of cloth boxer pants and a shirt. "How's a girl supposed to get laid wearing this?"

Kinji picked at it.

"Well, you could tie it up at the waist and maybe fray the pants."

"High fashion at the psych ward."

"It's a pharmaceutical center."

"Oh, pish." Tania sighed and got to work shimmying out of her clothes. She gave Kinji a hungry leer. "Ever done it in a, uh, pharmaceutical center, love?"

"No time, Tania."

"You, ma'am, are the definition of a drag." Tania pulled the pants on, then rolled the top over her head and straightened it. She glanced at Kinji and struck a pose.

"Well?"

Kinji stepped to her and planted a kiss on her lips.

"You're always lovely, honey."

Tania gave a satisfied groan. "Worth every minute."

Kinji rolled her eyes.

"Time for a diversion, right?" Tania said.

"Yes, I believe it is."

Tania shook her arms out, letting her own nerves settle. She was as nervous as Kinji but was hiding it behind her dope-addled sheen. The two of them went to the door.

"All right," Tania said. "You'll come get me, right?"

"Eh." Kinji shrugged. "I'll see if I can fit it into my schedule."

"Now, you joke?"

"Sorry."

Tania nodded. "I go left, correct?"

"Yes. Left, then down the hall, then right." Kinji put her hand on Tania's arm. "Good luck. Make a right-fine Tania Brae of a ruckus."

"Oh, baby doll, you know that's what I do."

Then Tania passed her hand over the security scan. The door opened, and she stepped out. Kinji slipped out behind her as the door slid shut, then headed right to Tania's left.

She needed to get around the loop and back to the security desk before Tania made her way from the other direction. She stepped quickly but tried not to appear hurried. She'd left her Think Space closed but knew that was no guarantee she was in the clear.

The pharmaceutical wing had a very different feel to it than what she'd seen while visiting Bexie Montgomery. Whereas the rooms she had been in with Montgomery had been open and invigorating places designed for comfort and learning, compartments here were spaced closely. The doors were simple and unadorned.

She turned a corner and just barely managed to avoid running into a nurse who was walking beside a patient.

"We are in a great place today," the nurse was saying.

The patient spoke the words back in a hushed tone.

He was gone, Kinji realized. His brain ravaged. Was it from an actual addiction, or — thinking about Bexie — had he been cut?

Ten paces from the security desk she slowed her pace.

Almost simultaneously a metallic crash came from the open area.

"Stop it!" Tania's voice rose in a shrill wail. "Stop it! I can't do this! I don't want to be here."

Sounds of a scuffle grew louder.

A security mech moved in, and the nurse staff went to their rooms. Kinji didn't hesitate. She pushed her way through the doorway into the nurses' center, then ducked down to slink past the open space.

There would be an access elevator in the next hall.

She saw three doors, two with full control panels and a third with a scanner lock.

She went to the lock and paused to jump into her private Think Space, where she dumped a piece of code into the processor. It was the inspector's sequence, and once it was running, she plugged it into her public node, then opened herself to the system.

This was her huge gamble.

For the next few seconds the system would see her as an inspector bot, but if she was still in this persona by the time the system registered duplicate sequences, the CIO would probably freeze her.

Kinji requested access, and the door slid open.

She stepped into the tube, and toggled the system to take her to Bexie's floor, dumping the inspector's persona as soon as the lift moved.

CHAPTER 31

Maine slipped through the access door without any problem.

He flipped on the flashlight embedded in his head wrap to find the corridor was spare and wide as it disappeared into the deep darkness. Tattered remnants of rat-chewed mattresses, flaking blankets, and torn cardboard were crammed into corners, century-old remnants of different days.

He walked slowly, picking his way and getting acquainted with the space.

Be a man, he thought, trying to calm his heart rate. Everything should be fine. Architectural documents said there shouldn't be cameras around, and the TS shield Pauli and DeJenna had given him should hide his approach. Still, he couldn't help being anxious. If he were caught... Well. He remembered the tone of DeJenna's voice as she let him know what a bad idea getting caught up in CIO business could be.

If she was afraid, he was afraid.

Add to that the heavy feel of the brick of plasta inside the utility belt hanging low on his waist, pressing against the small of his back. The belt made him sweat even more than his nervousness did. The sweat made the package shift and feel slippery as he moved.

Each time the brick moved he imagined another huge explosion.

He didn't like the sound of a creature scurrying away in the darkness, either. Pedrigo had laughed as he told stories about rats the size of Boston. Maine hoped Pedrigo had been kidding but he gripped the crowbar Pedrigo had given him tighter, feeling better knowing he had a weapon.

The hallway was six or seven meters wide, its graffiti-scarred walls lined with cobwebs and skittering insects. Looking at the graffiti made Maine recall a memory of cave paintings Jed Abraham-Jones had brought to the learning session a few months ago. Maine wondered who had painted them, and wished he'd paid more attention.

His steps echoed around him in a way that made him feel intensely alone. He waved the crowbar ahead of him as a spider ward. Hoping to remain quiet, he altered his gait. The act of placing his feet in the right spots helped take his mind off the bigger picture.

The cold blue LED flare of his headlight accentuated his tunnel vision.

Step by step, he progressed.

The ten minutes it took to make it to the old elevator shaft were perhaps the longest ten minutes of Maine Parker's life.

When he arrived, he pushed the crowbar into the slot between the doors, then leaned on it hard like Pedrigo taught him. They pulled open a bit. He pushed harder. Another couple tries and the door finally gave.

Sweat poured off Maine's brow as he looked up through the slot.

The blueprints had not been totally wrong.

The shaft had been left unfilled, but chunks of concrete and steel and plastic were piled up on the floor to the point where only a small crawl space was open toward the ceiling. Maine spent another ten minutes removing parts of desks, computer screens, and office walls, not to mention other crap he had no idea about.

He was breathing hard.

His arms and back hurt, and threads of muscle throbbed all the way up his forearms. These were different muscles than he usually used. He worried about whether he'd be able to run again.

When he glanced up, he saw space to climb.

"Worth every minute," he mumbled.

He slid the crowbar into a loop on his belt, and started to climb up the shaft, using service ladders whenever they existed and dangling cables when there was no ladder.

The going was extremely hard.

His arms and shoulders burned with every meter he gained. He wouldn't make it to the nineteenth floor — where the lock-down security servers were — if he'd had to shimmy up the entire distance.

He caught his breath for a moment, then twisted to get himself swinging to the next ladder. The light from his head band flashed on the wall as the cable creaked. He didn't want to think about what would happen if he slipped, didn't want to fixate on the furniture, glass, and other hard plastic crap that would impale him. He grabbed the rung, then latched his foot around the ladder, feeling his body settle in.

He rested again, letting the adrenaline-fueled tension that was pounding through his veins fade a bit.

An image of Beatrice came to him then.

Swinging out over the open shaft. Smiling. Saying she was going to beat him.

Her skin radiant.

Eyes bright and shining.

This was so much more than rock diving.

In other circumstances, even he might find some fun in the climb, but Beatrice would love it no matter what.

Either way, though, he could do without the pain.

The index finger of his right hand felt like it was on fire — either bruised or broken — probably just bruised, and his other hand was cramping. Nothing was going to stop him, though. He was going to make it.

He craned his neck to let the light play up the shaft.

More rungs created a stitched pattern into the darkness.

One step at a time, Maine Parker ascended.

Soon his movement had slowed to more of a lizard crawl than a climb, made even worse by the fact that his knee was beginning to boil with a hot pain. Every two floors he stopped to rest, pulling himself tight against the wall, not certain if it would be better to be in the dark rather than let the light strapped to his forehead illuminate the space.

The floors were each marked with a painted number.

He climbed to nineteen, swung his leg out to hook the ledge, then wedged himself between the door and the ladder.

He flexed his hands to get the blood flowing properly.

They were shaking now.

Muscles felt torn and strained.

He pulled the crowbar from his belt loop, and nearly dropped it.

Pedrigo said the door would pry, but in the shaft itself the angle would be tough.

Maine had practiced it several times, which was good because he didn't think he would have figured it out himself — it was at an oblique angle to his body, requiring him to raise his hands high. The bad part was that his hands were already barely functional. At least once the doors gave a bit he could simply lean in and use his natural weight as his lever.

That was the idea, anyway. At least it sounded good when he was sitting in the back room talking to Pedrigo.

He took a deep breath. No time like the present.

He pressed the crowbar into the slot, straining hard.

Finally, he heard a crack.

The door shoved open.

Leaning hard, levering his body against the wall of the shaft as a brace, the door slid a centimeter further.

Then another.

CHAPTER 32

The two women were gone, and for what seemed like millennia Bexie pressed hard on the barriers Kinji had built around him, pounding on barriers and screaming for release.

She'd called it a safe zone, made it feel like a haven, but as far as he could tell nothing was any different here than before. It was dark and isolated. He felt jailed. A macabre loop played through his mind.

"When will I get to my body?" he remembered asking.

"One step at a time," Kinji had replied.

"I don't understand."

"We're going to keep you here," Tania had said. "We're going to find your body."

Who was Tania?

"Don't leave me alone," he said as darkness closed over him again. He felt like a child, embarrassed and afraid.

"I need you to stay here for a while," Kinji's voice

came back to him.

It was like that for several more cycles. Still, though, as time passed, Bexie calmed. Each memory spawned more, each moment created a newer calm until finally Bexie Montgomery felt the part of him that could rationalize come together.

He remembered the plan.

Kinji and Tania were coming to San Francisco to slip into the facility and get his body ready before loading him back into it. They were trying to save him, trying to keep him whole rather than allow the CIO to strip him of everything that made him who he was. He remembered that now.

The Central Inspector's Office feared him.

He couldn't help but laugh.

"Like Humpty Dumpty?" he'd said to Kinji when he saw their plan.

But they didn't understand.

"An old story from when I was a kid," he'd said.

"I love stories," Kinji said.

"I'll tell it to you some day."

It wouldn't work, though. Even if she made it to his body, they would stop her. And if they didn't stop her, the CIO would simply hunt them down.

The first of the Three Laws flashed into Bexie's memory.

A robot may not injure a human being or, through inaction, allow a human being to come to harm.

The zeroth law followed immediately.

A robot may not harm humanity, or, by inaction, allow humanity to come to harm.

The essential conflict between these laws struck

him hard.

No, he thought. He was too dangerous. The controllers wouldn't let him go free. He saw that now. Kinji couldn't help him. And he saw more, too.

The world had made it to post-capitalism, and as much as it pained him to say it, the idea worked: automated workforces, resources distributed on demand. People were happy.

But they'd gone too far.

The controllers of this world wouldn't let him go free simply because he'd run. He wasn't afraid of the big risk, so he had to be "cut." Had to be adjusted.

And by helping him, Kinji, too, was putting herself on the line.

The realization felt like a razor to the neck.

There was something about Kinji Hall. A certain grace that infused her creativity. Kinji played on the edge of perception, it seemed. Where everyone else he'd met in his short period had been happy, Kinji Hall seemed to radiate an essence of freedom he hadn't felt anywhere else.

She delighted in change. She enjoyed risk.

If she failed...

The idea of her being destroyed hurt more than the idea of him losing this new life.

Sitting, contemplating, Bexie suddenly felt the gateway.

It was a crack.

Small.

Infinitesimal, but there.

A warp in the safe zone almost impossible to perceive, yet, when looked at from just the right dimension and with just the right motivation, was

obvious.
    He smiled.
    There was a way, he thought.
    Gathering himself, he knew what he had to do.

CHAPTER 33

Kinji found Bexie unconscious and lying on a composite slab, wearing cloth trousers and a thin shirt with only a thin blanket draped over him. The clothing was good. Enough to possibly get out of here ... if she could get him roused.

That was the key.

Reload his personality and get him on his feet enough to fake his way out.

"Bexie?" she said, reaching into his TS and feeling the gap between him and his previous self. The deed had already been done. If the overwrite didn't take, Bexie Montgomery would function when he woke but he would not be the dashing visionary he had once been.

The idea offended something deep inside her.

She split her tasking, working in TS to unlock the safe zone and put his original consciousness into his mind, while in physical she tried to rouse him.

"Come on, Bexie," she said again.

He gave a grunt and his arm fell from his chest.

Drugged.

The personality load dropped, and, with a great gasp, he blinked his eyes open.

"Come on. I don't know what they've got you on, so you've got to work with me."

As she slipped her arm under his back, he tried to help.

She pushed herself further into his TS, willing his body to stand with her, his weight nearly toppling her to the floor.

He could move, though.

Barely.

One step, then another.

Lurching toward the door.

They weren't going to make it. Not this way.

"I need you to stand on your own, Bexie. You hear me."

He moaned, but when she stepped back his weight nearly levered to the ground.

Fuck.

Got to push, though.

Arriving at the doorway, she pushed the controller to open it.

Standing there was a doctor bot, blue lights flashing, and a nurse wearing a pink and white uniform.

CHAPTER 34

With a final push, Maine Parker shoved the elevator doors open far enough to slip though. Panting, he saw by the flashlight that he was in a long passage — the ventilator ducts that ran above an office floor and below the core processing room of the LA Geo-Span center. He breathed a sigh of relief that they were as tall and wide as DeJenna and Pauli had promised — service ducts designed to pump air through the entire building, large enough he could walk freely. He pressed his lips together and took a last look at the crowbar before dropping it down the shaft.

A long time later, he heard it impact the pile below.

Then he made his way forward, stepping cautiously through the darkness, unable to miss the grimy sensation that came as his feet slid with each step.

The run back would be treacherous.

He blocked that thought for now, though.

Focused instead on simply putting one foot in front of the next. Focused instead on the processing room that ran above him and that connected the center to the rest of the world.

There, the central radio receivers and entanglement relays existed. There, the very few direct-line security paths that needed to exist were wired. There, too, memory resided — or, perhaps better said, prisons existed. There, inside the room that Maine Parker found himself walking under were the security computers — high-speed processors that ran code the CIO used to watch over other code, other blocks of memory stored in machines on the opposite side of the room.

Those code blocks were the cortical processes, the synaptic memory patterns, and the knowledge bases that mapped together to represent the base operating systems of millions of human beings.

Full systems saved away, memory systems intact and well preserved.

The passage was long and seemed even longer as Maine walked it with a slow, even gait, pausing to take in both places where the ductwork turned. He pressed the soles of his shoes over the flooring. Slick. He imagined blueprints as he went, Pedrigo pointing out important places.

There would be two cores.

He would have to do this right.

When he arrived at what he thought was the right place, Maine reached into his belt and extracted the brick of plasta. His hands shook as he cradled it. The lighting and the fact that his arms hurt made it hard to work, but he split the explosive along the crease like Pedrigo had shown him, then pressed one handful to the ceiling, and then the next.

He connected the two with a small controller, again just as he had practiced with Pedrigo.

Finished with the preparation, he glanced down the ductwork hallway.

Five hundred meters, and his muscles were flayed.

I'm not going to make it, he thought.

For an instant he considered leaving. Taking it all down and walking away, retracing his steps and leaving everything just as it was. It was possible the system wouldn't work, right? Possible that DeJenna and Pauli didn't know what they were doing, possible the system would fail.

Then the image came.

Beatrice again.

Flying in the sky above the reservoir.

Swallowing down fear, Maine Parker set the timer and waited for the green cycle to finish before pressing the actuator.

Then he ran.

His feet were light on the floor, but pounding, the sound of his steps echoing in the closed space. His eyes focused into the darkness ahead, his body aching but his discipline holding, his gait stretching, his chest rising with exertion, holding his hands at waist level, the light from his forehead making the scene jostle ahead.

The first corner loomed.

He edged to the side of the passage, then slowed a bit and twisted his body to lean in. The planting foot slid, and his body flinched as he crashed into the far wall, staggering, hands smashing into the flooring as he stumbled but still managed to press forward.

His legs pumped. Thighs burned.

He didn't bother to slow down at the second turn, and merely threw the meat of his shoulder into the wall, then bounced off in stride.

Running.

Still running.

He wanted to check his optical timer, but it was a casualty of the shield DeJenna had laid.

It crossed his mind that a minute would pass, and the explosion would burn his shape into the elevator shaft. That this would be the only thing that would exist to let anyone know he'd been here.

Out of the darkness came the finish line, vertical this time, the dark gap between the decrepit elevator doors.

Maine strained to lengthen his stride.

Pictured Lucifer Jones.

Twenty meters away.

Ten.

Five.

Behind him, the world ripped itself apart.

CHAPTER 35

The Central Inspector sat in an infinite processor, suspended in a web of pure energy. Tendrils came from within the controller, drifting in the core of Think Space like reeds in the depths.

"Do you know why I'm here?" Bexie Montgomery said as he entered, spreading himself thin. Even then he knew he could not win, that the Central Inspector was too big and too powerful to be defeated. It pulsed with a sense of righteous power that Bexie recognized in himself: The Central Inspector knew it was right just as Bexie himself knew that he, too, was correct.

He felt the structure of the Central Inspector so clearly then.

As befitting its base operational concept its controller was simple, its higher stages split into command centers — each of those then broken into a cascade of multiple executives and policy operatives. Under those elements were operations and logistics, connections to manufacturing plants and to construction centers, to agricultural systems, water management processes, and thousands of subcenters.

The whole was knit together by a communal kernel.

Intense shells of energy snapped in the emptiness between each element.

"You are beautiful," Bexie said, unable to stop himself.

And it was. The Central Inspector was a reflection of the society it managed, perfectly laid out, exquisitely structured to deliver exactly what human beings had strived for since the dawn of humanity itself: security, stability, a steady state of maximized human comfort.

During his first life, when his original body was born, he wouldn't have believed it.

But here it was. Ideal. The perfect controller.

Yet, it had gone one step too far.

Bexie brought all his thoughts into a single point, all his memory, all his processes, every pattern of thought that had ever passed through his cortex. He thought about his greatest triumphs and his biggest defeats. He brought up his memories of Kinji and felt how the flavor of her simple presence had made it so clear what he had to do.

"You cannot destroy me," it finally said.

"I'm not here to destroy you," Bexie replied as he formed himself into a single, streamlined sliver — a dart that soared through the core of Think Space toward the Central Inspector's fourth lobe, and plunged into the deep code space of the fourth core.

Crossing the barrier into the lobe seemed like

diving into a sun. Molecules burned. Atoms shredded. Particles raced through space in random patterns to catch in processor traces and memory grids. A memory flowed. A line reconfigured.

"I'm here to change you."

CHAPTER 36

An instant after the explosion, trillions of bytes began to transfer to the core communications center, which then relayed them into pubic space. Comm channels connected, information passed through personal identifiers.

Around the world, processing cortices in thousands and thousands of people — some sleeping, some eating with their families, gaming, entertaining, some working on new stories, or building a piece of furniture for their kids, some picking on each other, joking, trying to one-up the one-uppers, some making love, others skiing gently down slopes — thousands and thousands of people received a gift of themselves that unwrapped inside their minds and took hold once again.

When it was done, the initiator ran a final stage, destroying itself from code space.

In a small house in Los Angeles, two rebels shared champagne.

CHAPTER 37

Standing in the hallway, facing the flashing doc bot and the nurse, Kinji felt the full weight of Bexie Montgomery go dead.

At the same the ceiling lights pulsed once, dark to light, before blasting into a blinding white. As one, they shattered, exploding into clouds of glittering crystal that left the hallway in pitch dark.

Her TS died, then flickered back to life.

Emergency lights flickered.

A warning blared.

She saw the nurse running. The bot lay cold on the floor.

"Come on!" she screamed at Bexie, hauling him, pushing him, dragging him hard down the hall. He was heavy, though. Too heavy. Her back strained. His weight slipped farther from her.

She found stairs and dragged him further, holding him now only by the shoulder.

Sound of feet running down the hall came from the facility.

Voices calling about downloads.

"Emergency Protocol Red," a voice called out in her TS.

"Get up, Bexie!" she screamed as she pulled him down the steps. "Get the goddamned hell up!"

His arm slipped out of her grip and he slid down several stairs.

Kinji cursed.

Tears started to form.

"I can't do this alone!"

As she bent, a bout of vertigo hit. Her stomach felt like it was going to back up, and she fell to her knees. Her TS flashed, and a burst of adrenaline made her choke. She was free. "Oh, shit," she said, a shiver of understanding making her freeze up.

Kinji crawled to Bexie's side.

"What did you do, Bex? What did you do?"

But the slack expression on his face, the lack of response to prodding in TS, and the realization that she felt suddenly unencumbered was all she needed to understand where Bexie was and what he'd done.

Yes, she thought, recalling the fervor of his questioning about the CIO. If there *was* someone who could find a gateway to the Central Inspector, she wasn't surprised it was Bexie Montgomery.

And, yes, she *was* free.

Totally free.

She could feel the difference.

She wanted to laugh but couldn't. Wanted to scream but wouldn't.

Even me, she thought. Kinji Hall, defender of expression. A worm of anger grew inside. She'd been cut, and never even been aware.

Hurried steps came from the stairwell below. Security, she thought. Her heart spiked.

No. No. A wall of anger built inside her.

She wouldn't let Bexie end like this.

She stood up, taller and bolder. She pulled on her TS, formed a message, and made an open invitation. "If you're going to take me, everyone's going to see it for what it is," she screamed. Her fists clenched. Her jaw set.

At last the footsteps made it to her level.

"What are you waiting for, sweetie? Let's get the fuck out of here."

Kinji burst into tears.

It was Tania.

CHAPTER 38

Two strides from the elevator door, the ductwork behind him flashed in brilliant orange. The pressure wave lifted Maine into free air, his feet still churning, his arms flailing free.

His shoulder slammed the corner of the door. His hip. Spinning. Falling. Opposite knee crammed into hard steel.

The heat wave was next.

Intense. Burning, but without flame. Thank God, thank God, thank God.

Then he was falling.

His torso spun. His hand reached a rung but slipped.

Glass, he thought.

Steel pit.

Broken concrete.

He fell further. The light on his forehead flickered off ladder rungs and the lone cable that fell from above. He grabbed at it. Pain. Hands. Flayed. Back burned. Still falling. Tumbling now.

The light fell from his head to tumble down faster than him.

His foot crashed into the wall, rebounded from a rung. His back, the shirt burned from him now.

With one last gasp, Maine reached a hand out.

Caught a rung.

Held. Held. Shoulder wrenching in pain. Body crashing hard into brick. Fingers bloody. Slipping. Falling again but grabbing another rung with the other hand.

Gasping for air. Gasping. For.

Holding onto the rung as tightly as he'd ever held to anything in his life, Maine Parker scrabbled a foot to take a hold. He looked down. Three meters below, maybe four, his headlight had landed, and cast harsh shadows on the pile.

"Babe?"

The voice was distant in his TS, but certain.

"Beatrice," he replied.

CODA

Later, measured here in fractions of fractions, sitting in a field of pure light, elements of thought coalesce. Pieces of something that was once a human, that once made the human, but are now separate. Fragments of idea. Bits of emotion. Opinion. They clutch together, absorb into the nothingness and into the everything-ness that is and was and forever shall be the Central Inspector.

The body of Bexie Montgomery lay somewhere.

Far away or maybe near.

There is no space in the Central Inspector's Office, only time and ideas, requests and responses.

Bexie feels that sense of now as he removes his oneness from the smoldering core of proto mass. As the smell of ash fills time around him he sees the Central Inspector for exactly what it is.

"We can't change things," he says. "Can't protect them from who they are."

"You do not understand them as I do."

Bexie feels the lobe pulsing. Electrons twirl and

spiral, hiss a song of infinite permanence as they build in his thoughts. Somewhere in the song he understands a truth. Somewhere is the essence of power. What it means to be so human, to be so fixed on keeping each other from winning that he missed the obvious.

"No. I will never understand who we are," he says. Somewhere in the portions of his thought that are leeching away, he feels another truth, though. "It is our nature to avoid seeing what we don't want to see."

If you enjoyed these stories, find Ron's work at
http://www/typosphere.com

If you sign up for Ron's newsletter, you'll get a free copy of
Glamour of the God-Touched, Volume 1 of *Saga of the God-Touched Mage*.

http://www.typosphere.com/newsletter

YOUR FREE BOOK IS WAITING!

AMAZON Bestselling Dark Fantasy Author Ron Collins

A mage's apprentice.
Sorcerers on the hunt.
Unnatural magic of devastating power.

Garrick is a mage's apprentice, soon to be a
full-fledged sorcerer. The course of his life is
clear—he will be an apprentice, a mage, and then
a superior. But a tragic accident finds him wielding
a god-like power over life and death.

As rumors of mage war grow stronger, he learns
his future is not fated to be as simple as he dreamed.

amazonkindle nook kobo iBooks

"A riveting tale of magic, death, destiny, and power."
David B. Coe/D.B. Jackson
Author of the Thieftaker Chronicles

Acknowledgements

Thanks to my daughter, Brigid, for helping me get this book into shape, and her always fantastic thoughts on various story and design. Thanks to Sharon Bass, a beta reader who went above and beyond the call.

Thanks to my writing buddy, Lisa Silverthorne for being there from the beginning. Without her writing along with me, this one would have never existed.

And thanks, too, of course, to Lisa, for being there, and for all of the everything elses.

About Ron Collins

Ron Collins is an Amazon best-selling Dark Fantasy author who writes across the spectrum of speculative fiction. You can find his work at all major online retailers. With his daughter, Brigid, he is also editing anthologies in the Fiction River series.

His short fiction has received a Writers of the Future prize and a CompuServe HOMer Award. His short story "The White Game" was nominated for the Short Mystery Fiction Society's 2016 Derringer Award.

He holds a degree in Mechanical Engineering, and has worked to develop avionics systems, electronics, and information technology before chucking it all to write full-time, which he now does from his home in the shadows of the Santa Catalina Mountains.

Discover other work by Ron Collins at:

Amazon.com
Kobo.com
Barnesandnoble.com
Smashwords.com
Books2Read

Follow Ron at:
http://www.typosphere.com
Twitter: @roncollins13

www.ingramcontent.com/pod-product-compliance
Lightning Source LLC
Chambersburg PA
CBHW061653190726
48289CB00006B/1855